THE MYSTERIOUS WU FANG

in

THE CASE OF THE SUICIDE TOMB

A Gripping Detective Novel by Robert J. Hogan

That tomb had been sealed for a thousand years; its discovery was an archaeological find. But few guessed its horrible secret, or knew that a certain smiling yellow man wished to enter its portals . . . not to study the withered bones, but to capture the death germs buried there—deadly germs of a rare plague of madness which he meant to use to control the world!

LOOK FOR WILDSIDE PULP REPRINTS:

The Mysterious Wu Fang in

THE CASE OF
THE SUICIDE TOMB

by Robert J. Hogan

Published by:

Wildside Press
P.O. Box 301
Holicong, PA 18928-0301

www.wildsidepress.com

CHAPTER ONE

A Living Corpse

THROUGH the wide studio window of a newly-built penthouse six stories above the narrow, winding streets of Chinatown, the bright morning sun slanted down on a tall, narrow-shouldered figure reclining luxuriously in a heavily-carved chair which, like every other detail in the penthouse, reflected Oriental atmosphere.

The man had a long, pinched face with a very high forehead that gave evidence of its enormous mental capacity. Set well back on his head was an Oriental cap with a streamer that bobbed up and down as he ate breakfast from the round teakwood table before him. A yellow mandarin robe

embroidered with a dragon design hung loosely from his shoulders.

Wu Fang, the Dragon Lord of Crime, finished his meal and clapped his hands twice. Immediately, a Chinese attendant entered, gliding across the room with only a slight shuffle of his feet. He picked the table up and disappeared as quietly as he had come.

As though his departure had been a signal, another door opened and a girl glided in. She was dark-haired and of a strange exotic beauty. A tightly fitting frock of sky blue silk, simple in mode, clung about her graceful form.

There was fear in her large eyes—fear and desperate defiance; and also resignation. As though she had all but given up hope of a happier life.

Her delicate lips were set in a hard line which even in its desperation, failed to hide the sweet loveliness of the girl.

Wu Fang turned and let his green, slanted eyes rest upon her fondly. His cruel lips smiled benignly.

"You need have no fear, Mohra, my beautiful flower," he said. "Come here. I wish to look at you—closer."

Without uttering a word, the girl came over and stood before him. As his glowing eyes focused full upon her face, she seemed to lose some of her fear.

"I am well pleased, my beautiful one," Wu Fang went on. "I was afraid that the punishment I meted out might have spoiled your beauty. But you are now lovelier than ever. This trace of fear in your eyes is very bewitching."

The girl remained rigid and silent like a fine example of a master sculptor's art. Wu Fang reached out one of his long-nailed hands and took Mohra's right hand in it.

"You are forgiven, my little flower. You have been justly punished and have learned your lesson. We are going on together, forgetting the past and looking toward the future when you and I will be the rulers of all races—together."

Mohra's lips moved slightly. "Yes, Master."

Wu Fang shook his head.

"No," he murmured silkily, "perhaps you did not hear all I said, Mohra. I said all of the past is forgotten. You are not to call me, 'Master.' To you I am Wu Fang. Let me hear you say it."

"Yes—Wu Fang," Mohra breathed.

"That is better," the Dragon Lord of Crime smiled. "And now, my beautiful one, will you bring me the clipping from Monday's paper? I would like to read it again."

The girl bowed. "Yes, Wu Fang," she said obediently.

The yellow fiend followed her with his green eyes as she turned and left the room.

"It is a pity," he said sadly, shaking his head. "I didn't intend to break her spirit; she was too valuable to me as she was. Now she is my slave, where before she was my assistant."

Mohra returned to the sun-drenched room a moment later, carrying a newspaper clipping in her hand. She unfolded it and handed it to Wu Fang.

The green eyes of the yellow man took in the details of the heading; he smiled slightly when he read the name of the correspondent who had written the article.

SUICIDE TOMB TO BE EXPLORED
by Jerry Hazard
McNulty Syndicate Special Correspondent

Tombstone, Arizona.—Archaeological circles were stirred today by an almost positive confirmation to the legend of Suicide Tomb and final disclosures as to its exact location.

Sitting Fox, newly elected chief of the Hopi tribe, in an interview with this writer, revealed his ownership of a map, placed in his hands at the death of his grandfather, Chief White Deer, former ruler of the Hopis.

While the exact location of Suicide Tomb has not been made public, reliable authorities place it within 100 miles of Tombstone.

Sitting Fox further reveals that, despite the warnings of fellow tribesmen, the map is to be placed in the hands of Rod Carson, eminent young archaeologist and personal friend of the Hopi chieftain.

Plans have been made to begin excavation as soon as an expedition can be formed. Mr. Carson is reported greatly interested in this new venture and is confident of making many important discoveries.

Sitting Fox's personal interests lie in wresting the secret that has been sealed within the tomb for more than three hundred years. His aim will be to remove the cloud of superstition which the mystery has laid over his people.

The young Hopi ruler has been known to white men as Stephen Fox, under which name he was graduated with honors from Carlisle University.

WHEN he had finished reading, Wu Fang looked up at Mohra, who was standing motionless beside him.

"Do you know the significance of this, my little flower?" he asked, tapping the clipping gently.

"No," said the girl softly.

"You don't even know that the one you thought you loved wrote the story?" the yellow fiend demanded.

"I saw his name signed to it," Mohra admitted, "but did not read it."

"That is too bad, my lovely one," Wu Fang murmured. "It would seem that you are losing interest in him. Here, read the article for yourself."

The girl hesitated. "That is a command?"

"Yes."

Mohra took the paper resignedly and read it. The yellow fiend watched her closely. Her face whitened as she finished and her lips tightened slightly; but there was no other sign of emotion. She handed the clipping back to Wu Fang.

"What do you think now?" the yellow man asked.

Mohra shrugged her beautiful shoulders. "Nothing," she replied hollowly.

"Nothing!" Wu Fang exclaimed. "You do not see—but perhaps, my little flower, you have not heard the legend of the Suicide Tomb?"

"That is true," the girl admitted.

Wu Fang leaned forward. "My agents in the southwestern part of the United States and Mexico reported the legend to me, which goes as follows: Hundreds of years ago, a great plague seized the Aztecs in Mexico. To prevent it from spreading, the ruler commanded all those afflicted to be driven northward and sealed in a great circular tomb near what is now the border between Mexico and the United States. The ancestors of the Hopis dwelled among those cliffs at the time and so learned of the forced migration."

Wu Fang paused, eyeing the girl carefully. Mohra looked thoughtful for a moment, then shook her head.

"I do not see yet," she ventured, "why you are interested in the tomb, Wu Fang."

Wu Fang chuckled. "When I chose you as an assistant, I believed you to be clever. Much to my regret, you appear to be growing stupid." The yellow man folded his hands across his stomach and sat back in his chair. "You see, my little flower," he continued, "with this plague, at my command, I would be in a position to have certain demands of mine carried out."

Mohra stared at him. "Suppose you did kill all the people in the world, what of it?"

Wu Fang's cruel face twisted into a smile. "Of course I would not kill all the people in the world. I would kill just enough of them to strike terror to the hearts of those who would be permitted to live. Then you and I would rule over them."

"You have a plan for learning the location of this Suicide Tomb?" Mohra asked.

"Yes." Wu Fang nodded. "In all probability, I will require your help later on. At present, other agents are working on the case. Any moment they will bring a certain party here for questioning."

The girl's eyes widened in sudden fear.

"You need not worry, my lovely one," Wu Fang cooed. "I am not speaking of your friend, Jerry Hazard. However, I assure you, I would like nothing better than to get my hands about the throat of Val Kildare, the United States government man."

"Why," the girl asked, "do you not make your moves without considering Hazard and Kildare?"

"Without considering Hazard and Kildare? What do you mean? I cannot seem to dodge them. They arise before me like stumbling blocks in everything I do."

"Perhaps there is a reason," the girl suggested. "Have you stopped to think, Wu Fang, that whenever you began a new conquest, you considered first killing Hazard and Kildare? Suppose you forgot they are alive and go about this new task without a thought of them."

Wu Fang seemed to consider that suggestion for a moment. Then he shook his head; his narrow, bent shoulders shrugged as he chuckled, "No, my beautiful one. I have sworn to Chang Li, the God of ——? that I will kill them in the most horrible way possible. Do you understand?"

"Yes," Mohra whispered through stiff lips. "May I go now?"

Graciously, Wu Fang assented.

THE girl had just gone out of the door when a knock sounded from behind a heavy drape on the opposite wall. A light of anticipation appeared in the strange, green eyes of the yellow fiend. He turned his head and called softly, "You may enter."

There was the sound of a door sliding back into a panel, and a young man appeared. He was dark-skinned and had the tall stature and light blond hair of Nordic people. He was very calm, poised, as he stepped in front of the Dragon Lord of Crime and bowed low.

"The body of Stephen Fox will arrive at any moment," he announced.

Wu Fang's green eyes snapped: "Stephen Fox's body? What do you mean by that, Gunnar?"

The powerful young Scandinavian smiled: "I mean that we have followed your orders, Master. Stephen Fox is coming up any moment—in a casket."

"He is *not* dead?"

"No. He seems to be because of the drug we injected into his body. Master, do you think he will give you the information you seek?"

Wu Fang's eyes narrowed. "I think I can make him speak," he said slowly.

Another knock sounded on the panel behind the drape. Gunnar

turned quickly and flung back the curtain, disclosing two husky, brown-skinned Malayans. Each was holding a handle of a casket.

"Enter," Wu Fang commanded.

The two natives bore the casket forward, placed it on the floor in front of Wu Fang, and bowed.

"You may go," the yellow man said shortly.

The brown-skinned men glided swiftly and quietly back behind the drape whence they had come.

Wu Fang rose leisurely from his chair. "Open it up," he commanded.

After a few moments of turning screws, Gunnar lifted the lid of the coffin. A young man, dressed in a well-fitting suit of civilian clothes, lay inside. He had jet black hair, high cheekbones, and skin the color of a burnished penny. His body was fastened securely to the sides of the casket by heavy straps. He lay motionless, his black eyes staring up at Wu Fang.

The yellow fiend smiled down. "I am overjoyed to welcome you to my humble abode, Stephen Fox," he said. "Please accept my apologies for any inconveniences you may have experienced in your somewhat involuntary journey hither from the West. In a few moments you will be able to walk and talk again. Would you like that? Yes, I can see the answer in your eyes, although you haven't the power to nod your head."

Wu Fang clapped his hands twice, and a servant hurried to his side bearing a small tray covered by a towel. In the center of the towel lay a tiny hypodermic.

Wu Fang bared the wrist of the Indian, jabbed the hollow needle under the skin, and pressed the plunger. Then he replaced the needle on the tray and nodded to the servant, who disappeared immediately.

After a few moments, Stephen Fox began to stir. His hands and legs moved slightly, his eyes shifted. With apparent effort, he managed to ask: "Where am I, and who are you?"

"I am one of your friends," Wu Fang told him, smiling benignly. "My agents have saved you from the grasping hands of others who would have caused your downfall. You have been brought here so that we may discuss the excavation of Suicide Tomb."

The Indian stared at him defiantly. "You claim to be a friend. Why, then, do you speak to me while I am bound here in this casket? Why do we not face each other as man to man so that we may talk over these things properly? Are you afraid of what I might do if you let me loose?"

"No indeed, my friend," Wu Fang said. "There is no reason why you should not be released." He turned quickly to his Scandinavian aide. "Gunnar, release Mr. Fox at once and help him out of the casket."

With a few swift movements, Gunnar unfastened the straps that bound the Indian to the bottom of the casket, took the red man's arms and helped him out of the coffin.

"Now perhaps we can talk things over," Stephen Fox said, stretching his long-confined muscles. "Let us begin at the beginning."

"I have a proposition to make to you," Wu Fang said bluntly. "For a certain reason, I want to be the first to investigate Suicide Tomb. I will pay you much money for your grandfather's map showing the tomb's location."

The Indian stared at the yellow man for a moment in utter disgust. Then he shook his head slowly, decisively.

"No," he said, "the bequest of my grandfather is not for sale."

"But wait," Wu Fang hurried on, "I have not yet mentioned the price."

"The price," the young Indian chief told him, "makes no difference. You could pay me a million dollars, but I would still say no. There are some things more sacred to a red man than money."

Wu Fang motioned him to a chair.

"I beg of you to be seated," he said graciously. He brought out a box of long Oriental cigarettes from somewhere about his robe and passed them to the Indian. Stephen Fox took one and Wu Fang held a light for him. When he was puffing at it and Wu Fang had lighted one for himself, the Dragon Lord of Crime nodded to Gunnar and the Scandinavian glided noiselessly from the room.

"Now," Wu Fang said, "we can perhaps come to an understanding. When I tell you what I have in mind, I believe you will agree with me. From time immemorial, it has been the right of the yellow man to rule the world. But misfortune has always dogged his footsteps. It is my work, then, with the great order of Chang Li behind me, to bring the entire world under the subjugation of the yellow race. And here, Mr. Fox, is where you can be of help. You, who are a full-blooded Indian, do you realise what that means?"

Without waiting for the young Hopi chief to answer, Wu Fang continued: "It means, Mr. Stephen Fox, that you and your people shall rule your share of the world. Long, long years ago, the white man came to your shores. He tricked you, bought your valuable lands in exchange for worthless trinkets, drove you back into small areas that they now call reservations. You Indians are really descended from the yellow race. I can see it in your face and in your eyes. Thousands of years ago your ancestors split from the Mongolian race and came across the neck of land that joins what is now Siberia to Alaska."

Stephen Fox shook his head stubbornly. "You are wrong," he said decisively. "The Indians do not spring from the Chinese race."

"It will not be necessary to argue that matter now," Wu Fang said. "If you will help me win supremacy over the world, you and your people shall rule the United States."

"And how," Stephen Fox asked, "do you intend to get control of the world?"

"That," Wu Fang told him, "is why I am interested in the Suicide Tomb. According to the legend, the people in the tomb died of a strange plague. My desire is to learn of that plague, to experiment with it until I can bring it under my control. Then I will be able to dictate to every country in the world."

Stephen Fox was slowly rising out of his chair. "You are mad! You are insane! Do you mean that you would murder thousands of people in order to frighten the rest? By the great sun god, you are a devil! The white brothers have called my people murderers in the past, but they never would have thought of doing anything as diabolic as you suggest!"

Suddenly the remains of the long cigarette dropped from the fingers of the red man and he clutched at his throat as though he were strangling.

Wu Fang clapped his hands and Gunnar reappeared. The Scandinavian reached the Indian just in time to catch him as he fell. He pushed him into the chair he had occupied before and held him still.

The coal-black eyes of the Indian were glaring angrily at Wu Fang, and his lips moved soundlessly.

"You would not speak before." Wu Fang chuckled fiendishly. "Now it is too late. You and your people, I believe, are sun worshipers, but perhaps you do not realize the full power of the sun. In a few moments I will show you what real sun worship is."

The yellow fiend jerked his head to Gunnar.

"Bring him out to the garden," he ordered, "out into the sun. He will either talk out there or be made blind by the sun god that he worships."

With that, Wu Fang turned and made his way out of the door to the Oriental penthouse garden. He walked noiselessly toward the side of an arbor where the sun beat down fiercely.

"Now," he said to Gunnar, who was following in his wake with the Indian in his grasp, "stand him up with his back against the arbor and bind him there."

After Gunnar had swiftly obeyed this order, Wu Fang suggested, "Put a strap about his head to hold it back so that he may receive the full benefit of the sun. The drug from the cigarette will wear off very soon."

Gunnar hastily finished binding the Indian to the lattice, tying him so securely that he couldn't move a muscle. The sun was glaring down directly on Stephen Fox's face and he closed his eyes to protect them from the terrific heat.

"We will remedy that difficulty," Wu Fang smiled cruelly. He called one of his Chinese servants and gave him an order. "Bring the eye lid sticks. Four of them."

A moment later, the Chinese returned with four little notched sticks, each about a half inch long and notched at each end. With these in his hand, Wu Fang stepped before the helpless Hopi chief.

The drug was wearing off rapidly; already the Indian was struggling feebly against his bindings. The yellow fiend lifted one eyelid, opened it wide so that the eyeball seemed to pop out of his head. Then he placed one of the little props at each end of the eye, fitting the edges of the upper and lower lids into the notches so that the eye was kept open wide.

He repeated that operation on the other eye and then stepped back to survey his work.

To anyone but Wu Fang and his agents, the sight would have been hideous. Stephen Fox was bound there with his head tied so that it tilted back, exposing his black eyes to the blinding rays of the sun. He could neither turn his head away nor close his eyes against that terrific, blinding light.

Wu Fang seemed to be enjoying himself immensely. That benign smile grew wider and wider as he watched the Indian suffer. He moved over so that he was in the shelter of a clump of bamboo shoots and continued to watch the red man's stolid face twitch involuntarily from the searing pain.

After several minutes he walked back to his victim.

"It is a pity," he said, "that you must be subjected to such pain. Even now, your sight can be saved. Say the words and the eyelid props will be removed."

The Indian remained silent.

"It is useless to pretend that you are still under the influence of the

drug," Wu Fang went on. "I know that wore off some time ago. The sun is burning your eyeballs and you are in great pain. There are tears running from your eyes."

Stephen Fox spoke then. "It is not the pain," he said haughtily, "that causes the tears. It is the muscles and nerves of my eyes that I cannot control. Kill me if you wish, but I will not tell you anything."

Those last words of the Indian's rang out defiantly, but Wu Fang only smiled and shook his head.

"Kill you?" he said. "No, indeed. I would gain nothing by that."

The jaws of the Hopi snapped shut stubbornly. "Torture me until I die," he said through clenched teeth, "but you will never know."

"Very well," Wu Fang nodded. "It is nearly time for luncheon now, and it is warm out here in the sun. I will go into my penthouse and eat. I will come back after I am through. You will change your mind by that time."

"No," the Indian retorted, "I shall not change it."

*   *   *

AN hour later, Wu Fang glanced at the time. "The sun's rays have made him blind already," he said to himself. He pressed a buzzer set in the arm of his carved chair. The door opened and Gunnar entered.

"You will go at once to Tombstone, Arizona," Wu Fang instructed him. "It is more difficult than I had expected to gain information from this Stephen Fox. Does Mr. Carson know you?"

"No, Master."

"Good. You are to give him this recommendation." He handed the Scandinavian a slip of paper. "It is a testimony of your intelligent and loyal work with Doctor Anderson in his excavations in Egypt," he explained. "You are an experienced archaeological digger. Money is no object to you. You are interested only in archaeology and its development. Get the map that Stephen Fox gave to Rod Carson. If it is impossible for you to secure this map, then you must carry on as a digger. You must be one of the first to enter Suicide Tomb. You must examine all that is within it and send me word at once."

Gunnar nodded. "You wish to learn principally of the plague?"

"That is correct," Wu Fang said. "But remember this: Rod Carson is an outdoor man and in spite of his lean appearance, he is very powerful. He has never been defeated in a hand-to-hand battle. Do you understand?"

"I believe so," Gunnar replied. "Do I start at once?"

Wu Fang nodded. "There is another small detail. Before you go, see Kai Lu. He has some special baggage packed for you—certain poisons and two of my little beasts."

The Scandinavian grinned hideously.

"I believe your arch-enemy, Jerry Hazard, is in that part of the country," he said. "Is there anything I should tell him for you?"

"Tell him?" Wu Fang breathed, and now his green eyes glowed. "Yes, tell him that the poison and the little beasts are for him, but tell him this after you have used them. Is that clear?"

Gunnar's grin broadened as he bowed and replied, "Yes, Master."

Then the Scandinavian made his exit softly, and Wu Fang signalled for another servant.

"Ask Nee-Sa to come in," he ordered.

The servant left, and almost immediately a slim, Chinese girl glided into the room. Wu Fang's eyes ran up and down her figure appraisingly and stopped to dwell on her face. She was not strikingly beautiful, but there was a childish innocence about her that was particularly attractive.

Her voice was very gentle as she asked, "You called me, Master?"

"Yes, Nee-Sa," Wu Fang replied. "I have work for you. You have already proven yourself on one case, and in spite of the fact that you are very young, you have shown that you possess no emotions or nerves. That is well, Nee-Sa, for I have a very special task for you to do."

The girl's childish lips parted eagerly. "I am to kill someone?"

"Yes, Nee-Sa," Wu Fang nodded. "I think you will enjoy this very much. You have heard of Val Kildare, one of my most bitter enemies?"

The Chinese girl smiled slightly. "I have seen him several times," she said, "He is very handsome, Master."

Wu Fang scowled. "Do you mean that you could easily fall in love with him?"

"I would do whatever you ordered, Master," Nee-Sa bowed. "But since he is so good-looking, it would make my work of enticing him into your trap much more pleasant."

Wu Fang studied the Chinese girl thoughtfully for a moment. It seemed incredible even to him that such words could come from those childlike lips, that thoughts like those should dwell behind such innocent eyes.

"Sometimes, Nee-Sa," he said, "you astound even me. I have great hopes for you in my work. I have wondered sometimes that if the truth were known about your parentage, your strange nature might be traced there."

The girl bestowed her sweet baby smile on him. "If you ever learned of my parentage," she said, "you would probably find that my father was the devil and my mother a she-vampire."

"I haven't a doubt of it," Wu Fang admitted. "This is your mission. You are to find Val Kildare. I cannot tell you his whereabouts, but I do know that he is somewhere in the east, possibly in New York. All of my resources are at your disposal. Find Kildare, tantalize him, torture him, and then the death will come as soon as you are ready. But the death has already been planned. Come closer and I will explain how it is to be administered."

CHAPTER TWO

The Gleaming Face

JERRY HAZARD was snapped back to consciousness by the whispering of his name. It was twilight and he had just dozed off in his room in Mrs. Marshall's boarding bungalow on the outskirts of Tombstone.

"Hazard! Hazard! Hazard!"

He tried to locate the direction from which the sound came, but now that his eyes were open and he was fully conscious, the room was deathly still. He rose from the easy chair where he had been asleep and stood motionless, listening. The room was quite dark, but the last light of day filtered in through the windows, outlining the furniture in dusky shadows.

For some time, Jerry Hazard had experienced a complete letdown, a rest from Wu Fang and his agents. So much so, in fact, that he had turned his attention entirely to his reports for the McNulty Syndicate. As a result, this weird whispering of his name in the darkness struck him more forcefully than if he had been on the lookout for such a thing.

Now, as he stood there, his eyes sweeping the interior of the room and his ears straining for the sound again, he sighted something in the lower corner of the north window, something white. It was a pith sun-helmet. There was a face under it shielded by two cupped hands.

Again the whisper came. *"Hazard! Hazard!"*

Jerry recognized the man instantly. He was Rod Carson, famous young archaeologist and explorer.

He leaped to the window. "Lord, but you gave me an awful start," he said. "What is it?"

"Come out through the back door as quickly as you can," Carson said.

Hazard turned quickly. "I'll be right there."

As he made his way toward the back door of the bungalow, his mind was on Carson.

When he first met the young archaeologist, he had liked him. Carson seemed like a very ordinary sort of fellow. He had much the same build as Jerry Hazard—slim body, broad shoulders. But it was after hearing him talk and seeing him in action that Hazard realized here was a man stamped as a leader. He had but one consuming passion in life—archeology. To be the first to discover ancient tombs and ruins gave Rod Carson a greater thrill than anything else he could imagine.

His bronzed face was square-jawed, keen-eyed. His nose was not quite as nature had intended it to be; for the bridge was slightly flattened and broadened, testifying to the fact that his life as an explorer in far comers of the world had not been entirely smooth sailing.

He found him at the corner of the bungalow. Carson was holding his fingers to his lips.

"Come on," he said in answer to Hazard's questioning look. "I want to show you something."

Hazard followed toward a tall syringa bush on the outer edge of the lawn. As they crouched behind it, he heard the gravel walk, just beyond, crunch under heavy footsteps.

"See that fellow?" Carson asked.

Hazard peered through the bush. He saw a young, well-built, light haired man walking down the gravel path. He watched him stride through the dust along the gravel path until the houses farther down the sparsely settled block hid him from view. Then he turned to Carson.

"I'm afraid I can't see anything very strange about him," he ventured.

"I didn't expect you to," Carson replied. "The main thing I wanted to ask—was if you had ever seen him before."

Hazard nodded.

"Yes," he said, "I think I've seen him downtown standing on a street corner."

"That's not so bad then," Carson said. "If he's a native he's probably all right."

Hazard opened his mouth to ask the explorer what he was talking about but Carson raced on.

"Do you know a Doctor Anderson?" he asked.

Hazard frowned.

"Doctor Anderson?" he repeated. "The name is familiar. Why do you ask?"

Carson motioned toward the house.

"Come on in my room and I'll show you," he invited.

Still mystified, Jerry Hazard followed him back into the bungalow. When they entered, they found buxom, motherly Mrs. Marshall reading the newspaper. As soon as she saw them, she folded up her paper and laid it aside, preparatory to a comfortable visit.

"Well, I suppose," she said, "that I'll be losing you two boys tomorrow. I hear you're going on that awful digging expedition to look for the Suicide Tomb."

Carson smiled.

"Yes, Mrs. Marshall, we are planning to leave tomorrow morning after breakfast. But don't worry. I intend to keep my room here so I'll have a place to come back to now and then for a little rest."

Mrs. Marshall looked obviously relieved.

"Well, that will be nice," she said. "I was afraid I was going to lose both of you for good." Her ample bosom heaved as she sighed deeply. "Dear me," she said, "it does seem such a waste of time to be digging around for a lot of old skeletons. Brr! It makes me shiver just to think of it. But I'll be glad to save your room for you. By the way, who was that fellow who just came, Mr. Carson? Somebody that's going to work for you?"

"I think so," Carson nodded. "Do you know him?"

"Well," the woman said hesitantly. "Not exactly. But I do think I've seen him downtown several times. Are you going to take him on?"

Carson shrugged. "I haven't made up my mind yet."

"If it was me," Mrs. Marshall said, shaking her head, "I'd never hire him. He's got a bad look in his eye. And my good husband used to say—he was a horse dealer, John was—that I could tell a bad horse just by looking at his eyes, and I ain't never gone far wrong, judging humans that way either."

"Well, don't worry about it, Mrs. Marshall," Carson said as he moved toward the hallway that led to his and Hazard's rooms. "If we do take him on, we'll watch him."

"I hope so," the woman answered. She picked up her papers and resumed reading as the two men stepped into Carson's room. Carson passed Hazard a pack of cigarettes. They lighted up and relaxed in two easy chairs. The young archaeologist took a piece of paper from the table drawer and handed it to Hazard.

"That's the recommendation from Doctor Anderson whom this fellow worked for last," he said.

Instantly, Hazard recognized the name. "Oh, yes, of course," he said. "Doctor Anderson, the explorer. That's funny. I was thinking all the time of a doctor of medicine."

"Did you know him?"

"I interviewed him once when he returned from his excavations in Egypt. That was nearly two years ago."

"Anderson's dead now, isn't he?"

"Yes," Hazard admitted. "The newspaper boys tried to play up the story about the pharaoh's curse, but they couldn't make it stick. Anderson was on a hunting trip in the Adirondacks when he was stricken with acute appendicitis. They operated on him, but it was too late. My boss was rather sore about it. He said 'Why the devil couldn't Anderson have died of a strange heart attack or a broken neck so we could at least hint that it was the curse of a mummy?'"

Hazard glanced down at the letter again, thinking hard to remember dates. "Let's see," he said. "Anderson died a week after election; I remember my boss remarking that there never was any news after election, and he was mad because we couldn't make something sensational out of the doctor's death. That would be about November twelfth or fifteenth and this letter is dated on the thirteenth. That makes it okay That would be just about the time he went on his hunting trip in the Adirondacks. Let's see what he says."

Hazard's eyes ran down the typewritten sheet of paper.

"H'mm. The fellow's name is Gunnar Drugge, and he was an expert digger with the doctor for several years. He ought to make a good man for you, I should think."

"Yes," Carson said, "I think he'll fill the bill all right, but there's one drawback. Are you quite sure you've seen him around Tombstone recently?"

"I don't know," Hazard admitted. "That light hair and dark skin make a distinct impression that you remember easily, but I can't say just when I saw him."

"That's my trouble," said Carson. "Let me tell you what sticks in my mind. You remember the last time we saw young Chief Sitting Fox? He came to the bungalow; I was out but he waited."

Hazard nodded. "Interesting chap. I talked to him for quite some time before you came."

"Exactly," Carson said. "On my way back, a man passed me walking very rapidly, as though he were trying to catch up with someone. It was dark and I didn't get a look at him. But I would swear that he was Gunnar Drugge."

Hazard was aware of a tightening in his throat.

"Good Lord!" he breathed, "you don't mean—"

"You guessed it," Carson said. "The next day some of the Hopis came looking for Sitting Fox. They said he had disappeared. And we decided that he had been either abducted or killed for the map—which, fortunately, he had already entrusted to me. I'm becoming more positive every minute that Gunnar Drugge had something to do with Sitting Fox's disappearance."

"What are you going to do about hiring him?" Hazard asked.

"Do?" Carson demanded. "I've already done it. I told him to report for work tomorrow morning at eight o'clock."

"I see," Hazard said with a smile, "that you're one of those fellows who believe in keeping your danger where you can watch it."

"Right." Carson nodded. "If he's just a good digger and hasn't anything to do with this, I can use him very nicely; and if he's mixed up in the death or abduction of Sitting Fox, then I want him where I can keep an eye on him."

Rod Carson fell silent. He lit another cigarette and leaned back in his chair, staring thoughtfully at the ceiling.

"It's funny," Hazard ventured from his chair near the open window, "that whoever wants that map doesn't attack you."

Carson smiled. "That's another thing I've wondered about."

Suddenly, Jerry leaned forward, wild thoughts were racing swiftly through his head.

"Do you suppose—" he started to ask. Then he stopped short and relaxed. "No," he finished, "I guess my imagination is getting the better of me. That idea doesn't click at all."

"What idea?" Carson demanded.

Hazard lowered his voice almost to a whisper as he replied, "You'll probably think I'm crazy, but have you heard of Wu Fang?"

"Is there anyone who hasn't?" Carson smiled. "He's a great friend of yours, isn't he? And of Kildare? By the way, where's Kildare now?"

"He's doing some secret investigating in New York."

"Hiding out?" Carson guessed quickly.

"Well, not exactly. I can reach him at any time through the Bureau. But to get back to my hunch. Wu Fang has the most astounding spy system in the world. His agents are everywhere. Suppose, for instance, that this Gunnar Drugge is one of them. You can easily imagine the rest."

By now the twilight outside had vanished; it was pitch dark. Carson rose and switched on the electric light.

"You know, Hazard," he frowned. "I can't agree with you on one thing. Wouldn't it be—"

Suddenly, Jerry leaped to his feet with a warning, "Sssh!" His hand stole under his light tropical suit coat for the automatic in the shoulder holster. Then he groaned with disappointment. He remembered that he had taken it off earlier that day because of the heat and laid it on the dresser in his room.

"I'd swear I heard a sound outside that window just now," he said softly. "I think someone has been listening to us."

"What?" demanded Rod Carson. He charged toward the window. Hazard caught him, tried to hold him back. "I wouldn't do that," he advised. Carson jerked away. "You mean I've got to be careful about looking out of the window of my own room," he demanded. "Nonsense!" And deliberately he walked to the window, stuck his head out.

"There's nothing here—" His words were chopped off as though an axe had severed them. He drew back; there was a bewildered expression on his face. "That's funny," he said in a rather hesitant voice that was not at all like his usually firm tone.

"What's funny?" Jerry Hazard demanded.

"That out there," Carson said.

"Yes, I know," Hazard probed impatiently, "but what was it? What did you see?"

Carson looked blank; his eyes had suddenly become those of a dreamer.

"Why—why, nothing."

"Well, what did you feel then?" Hazard demanded. "For heaven's sake, man, can't you remember?"

"Yes, I remember all right," Carson said as he got a grip on himself again. "Something brushed past my cheek—like a cool hand caressing me. It stroked my face once and then passed on."

"You can't say," Hazard grinned, "that I didn't warn you."

"No," Carson admitted. "You did your best but I was too pig-headed to take your advice. I've never run up against anything that a couple of good socks in the jaw wouldn't settle, but this is different. You can't fight anything that you can't see." He laughed a little nervously. "I'll be talking like a lunatic next," he said, a little sheepishly.

"You'll be all right when you get the hang of it," Hazard assured him. "I'm positive now that Chinese devil is in on this thing."

As he spoke, he saw Rod Carson turn with a jerky motion and stare

out into the night again. The archaeologist tensed and then leaped toward the table. With one swift movement, he jerked a gun out of the drawer.

Just outside the window, perhaps three feet away, was a face, apparently hanging in mid-air. It was faintly illuminated by the reflection from the electric light. It was pinched and drawn like the shrunken face of a mummy. Its protruding jaws looked like those of an ape and the wicked little deep-set eyes glared murderously at the two men.

Carson pulled the trigger of his gun. Flashes of flame shot out.

Blam! Blam! Blam!

The little bungalow shuddered as though an earthquake had shaken it. Then above the booming of the gun sounded a piercing scream of mortal terror.

CHAPTER THREE

Death Strikes

A HUNDRED and one things seemed to be happening at the same time. Jerry Hazard was vainly trying to locate the direction from which the scream had come and hold on to Rod Carson as he lunged toward the open window. The awful face had vanished completely.

Carson broke Hazard's hold, leaped to the window. In spite of his better judgment, Hazard followed. His keen eyes caught something moving in the night. He clutched Carson's shoulder.

"Look out there! Get it!"

Carson swung his gun in that direction. *Blam!*

The revolver exploded, letting go its last cartridge at a bent figure clad in long, flowing skirts. The figure disappeared around a shrub near the front of the house.

This time Hazard acted first. He lunged forward and jumped out of the window, landing on his hands and knees. Carson came charging down on him. Then they raced for the spot where that mysterious figure had vanished.

From inside the house came the sound of slippered feet.

"Boys!" Mrs. Marshall called. "What's wrong?"

Hazard stopped long enough to answer in a voice just loud enough to reach the woman's ear. "We're all right. Go back to bed. I'll explain later."

A FEW moments later, the chief of police, who comprised the major part of the Tombstone police force, loomed out of the darkness, yelling at the top of his voice.

"What's all the shooting about?" he demanded.

They told him what had happened and he joined in the search— a search that ended at midnight without success.

When they arrived back at the bungalow, they found the front door bolted from the inside and started to walk around to the back.

Hazard stopped abruptly outside Mrs. Marshall's bedroom window. There were sounds coming through the opening, sounds of a bed creaking and of muffled sobs.

"Quick!" he shouted. "Something's happened to Mrs. Marshall!"

They raced to the back door, lunged down the hall. Hazard was the first to reach Mrs. Marshall's room.

The elderly woman was lying on her bed clad in a flannel nightdress. Her hands and feet were bound with a piece of clothesline; one of her own stockings was stuffed into her mouth and the other was tied around her head to hold the gag securely in place.

Hazard and Carson quickly unbound her.

"If I ever get my hands on her, I'll show her," she fumed.

"Her?" Carson demanded.

"Yes, sir, that's what I said. If I ever get my hands on her—or maybe it was a him dressed in woman's clothing. A few moments after you boys went out, I heard somebody at the back. A woman in a long old dress, something like the ones my grandmother used to wear, burst in. I tried to yell for help but she clapped her hand over my mouth and started to tie me up."

"Did you see her plainly?" Carson asked.

"No, I couldn't get a good look at her face. She got me all tied up with my own clothesline and gagged me with a pair of my stockings. They were a dirty pair of stockings, too. I tried to tell her that if she was going to put stockings in my mouth to get a clean pair out of the drawer, but she wouldn't listen. Then she left me and went in your room, Mr. Carson. I heard her rummaging around and pulling out drawers."

Hazard whirled suddenly to Carson with a cry of alarm. "Carson! that map! Have you—did you leave—"

Carson gave a short shake of his head, "Don't worry about the map," he said. "It's okay. Come on, let's see what they've been doing in my room."

They left Mrs. Marshall still sputtering and fuming and went into Carson's room. A scene of wild disorder greeted them. The bedclothes were shaken out and heaped in one corner. The mattress was upturned and slit in a number of places. Drawers were pulled out and their contents spilled all over the carpet, which had been rolled up. Carson's baggage was strewn about the room as though it had been hit by a hurricane. Even the pockets of his clean shirts had been searched.

"Well," the young archaeologist ventured, "they certainly make a good job of it. I wonder if they went into your room, Jerry."

Hazard was already at the door of his own room. He snapped on the light; the same general disorder faced him. Everything had been gone through with the thoroughness of a fine-toothed comb. He turned just in time to see a smile of amusement cross Carson's face.

"I'm glad you can take it with a grin, Carson," he said rather coldly, "but I can't see anything very funny about it."

"I was just thinking," Carson chuckled, "what a whale of a lot of trouble somebody has gone to. I imagine she—or he—would be sore to know I had it in my pocket all the time."

Hazard stepped over to the window and closed it before he answered.

"I imagine she's delighted to have you tell it," he said crisply.

"You don't mean that someone is outside now, do you?" Carson demanded.

"I don't doubt it in the least," Hazard said.

Carson shrugged. "I don't suppose it really matters," he said indifferently. "They'll probably get the map before they're through in one way or another."

"Yes," Hazard nodded, "and they'll get you with it. I'm not trying to frighten you, Carson, but it might be well if you took a little more precaution."

They turned as they heard the sound of shuffling feet in the hall. Mrs. Marshall appeared in her bathrobe and slippers.

"Mercy!" she exclaimed as she surveyed the upset condition of the room. "I had no idea that they'd messed things up like this. You boys get out of my way now and I'll make up your beds again."

WHEN Jerry Hazard retired, his brain was filled with vague apprehensions as he lay there on his freshly made-up bed. His mind flashed from one thought to another. Finally, a fitful, troubled sleep stole over him. Horrible creatures of Wu Fang's breeding appeared before him. There was a barbed-tailed lizard and a rat-headed serpent with large scales on its body and tail.

Subconsciously, he realized that he had made a mistake. He should have made a thorough search of his and Carson's room before they turned in for the night.

He struggled to wake up but he didn't seem able to surmount the fog of sleep that gripped him. He tried to cry out but he knew that no sound left his lips. Suddenly he grew cold with terror. For he realized at last the significance of what had happened several hours ago when Carson leaned out of the window. Wu Fang's agent had annointed him with the death odor—the odor which would attract the tiny death beasts!

Hazard was fully awake now. He was staring fixedly at the ceiling, ears straining to catch a sound that he couldn't quite define, a strange, soft rustling. His right hand crept under the pillow and grasped the revolver that was there. He was ready now. Let them come on and get it over with.

But the sound had ceased, the air around grew deathly still. It seemed almost as if someone had sensed his awakening and withdrawn.

Seconds dragged by like hours. Twice he was tempted to get up and switch on the light, but his better judgment prevented him. Perhaps his suspicions were silly. Perhaps there was nothing outside the window. He had just about decided that it was all a combination of the wind and his overworked imagination when the sound came again.

He drew out his automatic, and again the sound ceased abruptly. From far off came the lonely howl of a wolf. A moment later the howl was answered by another eerie bay, then suddenly a cry sounded from closer range. It was low and muffled and sounded more like a grunt than anything else. It came from the room where Rod Carson slept. He heard a sharp creak, then a slight squeak, such as a mouse might make.

Jerry Hazard raised himself cautiously on one elbow. He had one foot out from under the covers, ready to step on the floor, when he froze abruptly. Through the open window something was moving, something ghostly in appearance. An arm came up; behind it another shapeless mass arose—a second arm.

Hazard's thoughts flashed to articles he had read on spiritualism, on the substance called ectoplasm; he noted the resemblance between that and this filmy stuff that floated in through his window. As he watched, the ghostly substance assumed a definite shape. He distinguished a pair of shoulders and the upper part of a body. But there were no legs or feet and most ghastly of all, no head!

The white mass was rising higher and higher, holding Jerry Hazard spellbound as he watched it with staring eyes. Cold sweat was pouring out on his forehead and a lump that had risen in his throat seemed to be choking all the breath out of him.

The ghastly, shapeless white mass was floating toward him, wavering slowly back and forth as though it were alive.

Hazard raised his gun to fire. The swaying white phantom was not more than six feet away now. He pulled the trigger.

Blam! Blam! Blam!

The bungalow echoed with the deafening roar of his gun. In the spurts of flames he saw that the phantom visitor was transparent. As his bullets found their mark, the ghostly thing ceased weaving. It leaped high into the air, then shot toward the window. It hovered there a moment and then—right before his eyes—vanished completely.

The newspaper man leaped out of bed, fumbled for the light switch, turned it on. Then he ran to the open window and peered out. The next moment he ducked back inside again, raced across the floor, and plunged into Carson's room. A body hurled at him. He ducked. He had only his bare fists now.

He made a wild guess at where the head of his assailant should be and let go with a right and left that had all the power behind them that he could muster. His opponent was hurled back. Hazard, giving him no chance to recover, followed up with a terrific series of blows. Suddenly the room was flooded with light.

WHEN he entered that dark bedroom, Jerry Hazard was positive he would find Rod Carson either knocked out or dead. That sickly squeal had probably issued from one of Wu Fang's tiny little death beasts.

But when the electric light suddenly flooded the chamber, Jerry saw that he was wrong. Rod Carson was standing at the open door, hand still on the switch. And the only body in evidence was that of a small beast lying perfectly still and lifeless.

Carson smiled sheepishly as he straightened his pajamas and felt of his jaw tenderly.

"Boy, Hazard, you've got a sock like the kick of a mule," he said.

"Well," Hazard admitted, "I guess anyone could put a lot of force behind his blow if he thought he was tangled with an agent of Wu Fang."

"That's pretty good." Carson nodded, joining the newspaperman in a nervous, relieved laugh. "We each thought the other was one of Wu Fang's agents." His eyes narrowed as he looked at the little beast on the bed.

"What in the name of heaven is that?" he demanded. He stopped short, frowned. "I am beginning to remember now. I had a dream. In my dream something brushed my shoulder and started crawling up toward my cheek. I reached up with my hand, grabbed something and squeezed it with all my might. It squeaked and then I threw it away from me. The next thing I knew, I heard shots coming from your room and I woke up."

"Do you actually mean to say," Hazard demanded incredulously, "that you killed that little death monster without realizing it?"

Carson shrugged, leaned over the bed, and reached out a hand for the still little form. Hazard grasped his wrist.

"I wouldn't touch it," he said.

Carson took his advice and stepped back.

Jerry Hazard picked up his automatic from the floor where it had fallen and, with the muzzle, probed the still body. The beast possessed characteristics of several types of reptiles and lizards.

It was four inches long, including the short, stubby tail that was heavily armored with scales. The entire back was covered with a heavy, barbed shell from which four fairly long legs and a head—it was not unlike that of a miniature sea horse—extended.

The thing didn't move as Hazard poked it. He managed to get the muzzle under it; balancing it dexterously in that manner, he lifted it up very carefully and laid it on the table directly under the light.

"I'm quite sure, Carson," he remarked, "that you killed it. But we've got to be certain."

"I never saw any animal like it," Carson said.

"I know of only one place in the world where beasts like this can be found," Hazard told him. "That's in the private breeding laboratory of Wu Fang."

"You mean Wu Fang crossbreeds lizards, turtles, serpents, and that sort of thing?" Carson demanded.

"Yes, and that's not even a beginning of the fiendish hybrids he creates."

"But why would this little thing attack me?"

"It's quite simple, as my friend Kildare explains it," Hazard said. "These beasts are controlled by their sense of smell. Wu Fang and his agents make themselves immune by anointing themselves with the odor that repels them. If a person is anointed with an odor that attracts them, they will attack him instantly."

Carson looked puzzled, shaking his head.

"Remember when you felt something brush your face earlier tonight?" Jerry continued. "The agent was probably hiding in the shrubbery outside the window, just waiting to anoint you with the attracting fluid. It could have been done in several ways. He might have doused a small swab into the liquid, tied it to a string, hit you with it, and then pulled it back before you could see it. Or he might have squirted it from a bulb gun."

Carson's eyes lighted at this suggestion.

"That's it," he said. "That's exactly what it felt like—a thin, cool spray that touched me lightly for only a minute."

Hazard was pointing to the long, thin neck of the little beast.

"You must have caught him by the neck and choked him to death," he guessed. "That's the only place where you could have done it."

"I suppose so," Carson admitted.

"And the squeak that I heard," Hazard finished, "was the last gasp of the beast." He turned toward the door. "The two of us seem to be okay. But I'm wonder ing about Mrs. Marshall. With all this commotion going on she should have awakened."

He stepped out into the hall, tapped lightly on Mrs. Marshall's door. There was no answer. He knocked again. Silence reigned. A queer dread clutched at his heart. Before he could speak Carson shouted: "Look out!"

At the same time he leaped back and began stamping the floor like a Hillbilly doing an old fashioned hoe-down. Under his feet, a wriggling form moved with lightning speed—striking, coiling, and striking again.

Bam!

Carson stamped hard with the heel of his slipper. A cry of triumph leaped from his lips.

"Got him!"

He continued to grind the head of the serpent tinder his heel. The rest of the body wriggled. But that meant nothing, for the head was crushed. At last Carson stepped away. He and Hazard surveyed the wriggling reptile.

It was not more than eight inches long and had an extremely thick body for its length. The skin was a dull gray brown that would make it difficult to see in most places.

Hazard knew the answer without even opening Mrs. Marshall's door. There was no need of knocking now. He turned the knob and pushed the door open.

"The little devil was coming under the door, heading for me," Carson panted. "I suppose he smelled the attracting perfume on me."

Hazard nodded. He was fumbling for the light and his hand was a little shaky. At last he found the button; the room was flooded with light.

The two men bent over the still form of Mrs. Marshall. She was lying on her back. Her mouth was open, as though she had tried to cry out just as she died.

Hazard pointed to a pair of tiny pin pricks just under the left side of the chin. He couldn't speak. Then silently he drew the sheet over the face of their late housekeeper. He turned out the light, and they went out into the hall.

"I'll report this to the authorities when we get to town at daylight," Jerry said. "There's nothing can be done before then."

Carson nodded. "I hope you're not going to propose that we go back to bed and try to sleep."

Hazard shook his head.

"Hardly," he said. "We've had all the sleep we're going to get this night I suggest we get dressed and then, as soon as it is light, go outside and have a look around."

Jerry Hazard dressed rather nervously. Upon returning to his room he had intended to close the window. But he decided against it. He took out his automatic and surveyed the interior.

So far as he could see, nothing had been touched. But that didn't mean that beasts of death might not be lurking in dim corners, or even in the folds of the bedclothing, hiding there to strike when he came near enough.

Using his automatic muzzle he began poking about. After that experience in the hall, he was jumpy, and he feared the sudden lunge of a beast or reptile.

One by one he shook out the blankets and sheets. Standing as far away as possible, he moved his suitcase–his typewriter–searched under the bed.

Satisfied, in part, that there were no poison beasts here, he began to dress. And here again he used utmost caution, shaking out his clothing, turning things inside-out and back again before he put them on.

And always he tried to keep an eye on that open window. For out there, somewhere in the darkness that was deepest now, just before dawn, lurked a messenger of death. A marauder that killed as he searched. A murderer, who sought a chance to get the map that Rod Carson held concealed.

Hazard was seated on the edge of the bed, tying his shoe, when he heard a sound outside. Instantly, his hand snatched the automatic that lay beside him, ready cocked.

His eyes swept the blackness. A blurred object was hurtling at him. Instinctively, he leaped to the side. A second later he grinned in relief.

A crumpled bit of white paper had bounded into the room and rolled to a stop at his feet.

Without waiting to pick it up, he leaped toward the window, careful to keep his body shielded. He had caught the line of travel taken by the paper wad.

His automatic poked out into the night. The sounds of running feet came to him. He fired after them as fast as he could pull the trigger.

The pattering feet died away. There was no sound except the echoing of the shots he had fired.

Carson came diving through the door. "What the–" he began. Then he stopped short as he saw Hazard picking up the paper from the floor.

He unfolded it cautiously, holding it by a corner at arm's length. No, there was nothing hidden in it–no tiny, deadly reptile. He and Carson stared at the words.

YOUR TIME HAS NOT COME, HAZARD.
BUT IT WILL BE VERY SOON.

"I must say," Carson exploded, "that's cheerful."

"Yes," Hazard agreed, "it does make me feel relieved. At least I know I've got a little while to live."

AS SOON as it was light, the two men emerged from the bungalow and hurried around to the garden under the windows of their two bedrooms.

"Keep a lookout," Hazard warned. "Someone might still be lurking about. I'll make an inspection here."

The newspaper man began searching about in the soft earth under his window. His eyes widened as they spotted something in the dirt.

"Look here!"

He was pointing down at a huge track, a track that was not unlike a human hand except it was much larger.

"Good heavens!" Carson exploded. "It looks like a giant's handprint."

"I thought you'd recognize it," Hazard said. "You've been in Africa, haven't you?"

"Yes," Carson nodded. "I know what you're thinking of. And you're right. It's the track of a gorilla. Do you think that a gorilla is responsible for some of the things that happened tonight?"

Hazard shrugged. "We could spend the rest of our lives standing here, talking about it—and we wouldn't get anywhere. I'm going to wire Kildare."

"What are you going to tell him?"

"That Wu Fang is interested in the Suicide Tomb!"

CHAPTER FOUR
Suicide Tomb

It seemed incredible to Hazard, as he sped along the smooth desert road in the crisp morning air, that only a few hours before, death had stalked this peaceful country. Mrs. Marshall's tragic fate had cast a mantle of terror over the community.

The sheriff had cooperated with them in releasing the story that a rattlesnake had killed her. But too many people had heard the gun shots the night before; several persons claimed to have seen a gorilla stalking through the shadows; tales of deadly serpents, of ghostly shapes, of weird cries for help began circulating. And somewhere—someone—got the name "Wu Fang." Had Wu Fang come to Arizona? Was he even now hidden nearby, ready to spring a new horrible death upon the world?

Hazard was glad that he had wired to Kildare before the archaological party left Tombstone. If the secret service agent was in a place where he could be instantly reached, he should arrive here tomorrow morning at the latest. Jerry breathed a sigh of relief. For he knew that Val Kildare was the only white man in the world who could hope to balk Wu Fang's schemes of murder.

There were ten assistants in the party, including Gunnar Drugge. The Scandinavian's expert help had began to dispel Hazard's suspicions. Now, as they rode in the same open car, he wondered that Carson and he had doubted this likeable young fellow. When they pitched camp at noon, he watched with favor Drugge's expert handling of the other men.

Nevertheless, Hazard still had the feeling that among that party of laborers were one or more agents of Wu Fung. Two of the Mexicans had shifty eyes. But Rod Carson said he trusted them because they had been with him on another excavation project in Mexico. Hazard felt a touch of guilt as he watched the Chinese cook prepare the noonday meal beside a narrow canyon; but nevertheless, he spoke to Carson.

"I suppose," he said, "it's foolish of me, but I'd like to know all about the Chinese cook."

Carson laughed. "I'd bet on him against any of the rest. He's not only the best cook I've ever had but he's as honest and faithful as they make them."

Hazard let it go at that, but he continued to watch the members of the expedition.

When the noon meal was finished, they broke camp and moved on. About three o'clock, they stopped at the entrance of a wide valley which was dotted with growths of sage and cactus on either side of a swift river that raced through its center. To the north, a series of cliffs towered for more than a half mile above.

Hazard's attention was directed toward those monstrous cliffs. In those great recesses, built on wide ridges of rock, were remnants of the ancient cliff dwellers' art.

Rod Carson strode out into the sage brush; Hazard joined him.

"Is this the place?" he asked in a low voice.

"I think so," Carson nodded. "Yes, there's the watcher's little dwelling. We can walk up to it. See, there's the trail."

"I see what you're pointing at," Hazard said, "but I don't know what you're talking about. What is a watcher's dwelling?"

Carson looked grave. "As you know," he explained, "those afflicted with the plague were sent here from what is now Mexico. The Hopis were drilling up there in the cliffs of that great white ledge. See it?"

Hazard nodded.

"The Hopis thought they were being attacked," Carson continued, "so they built fires on the cliff edges and dropped brands. In the light of those firebrands, they saw several hundred people being driven up that path to that narrow shelf of rock; suddenly the mob vanished. There was no way for the Hopis to get down and see what was going on before morning; by then, the cave was closed up. They heard strange sounds through the crevices in the cliffs for days after, and believed that evil spirits dwelt there. So they built that watcher's hut and picked the bravest man of their tribe to live there and kill the evil spirits whenever they should come out."

"The Hopis knew there was a cave, then?"

"Apparently. But either they couldn't move the huge stone that had been dropped over it to seal the entrance—or they forgot where the entrance was."

"What do you plan to—"

Hazard's query was cut short by the snap of a twig behind them. Carson must have heard it too, for he spun around, hand darting for his gun. But even as he reached for that weapon, a man stepped out of the brush, and they saw that it was Gunnar Drugge. He was bending over, staring down at the ground. Suddenly he lifted his blond head.

"Excuse me," Drugge said politely, a quick smile crossing his face. "I was looking for firewood. Do you wish us to pitch camp here, Mr. Carson?"

Carson nodded. "We'll make camp at the side of the road where the cars are now."

Drugge bowed with a polite, "Yes, sir," and moved away. He held a few sticks in his arms.

Hazard watched him go intently. "Funny," he said. "Did he know we were going to camp here?"

"No," Carson said, "I hadn't told anybody."

"Then why," Hazard demanded, "would he be looking for firewood?"

"Probably," Carson said, smiling, "so that he would have a good excuse for listening to what we were saying."

"You don't trust him any too much, do you?" Hazard asked. "Neither do I. I like your idea of keeping him here where we can watch him."

When they returned to the cars, they found that the crew of workmen had already begun to pitch camp under Drugge's orders.

"Well, at least his work can't be criticized," Hazard remarked. "I suppose you're going to wait until tomorrow morning to start operations."

"No," Carson replied. "On the contrary, we're going to start very soon. As a matter of fact, while they're pitching camp, you and I are going to climb up this path of the first ridge and take a look around."

THEY found the watcher's adobe hut on the edge of the lower cliff shelf partly in ruins. It had probably been like that for hundreds of years. Carson paid little attention to its neglected condition but strode on around it.

Hazard kept close behind and also maintained watch down the trail. No one had followed them up here. The only way to approach the spot was by way of the trail, and that was plainly visible from the top of the ledge.

Huge rocks lay here and there against the blank face of the cliff where they had fallen from above, loosened by the ravages of weather over hundreds of years. Carson stopped before one particularly large slab and studied it intently.

"This doesn't look much like a job for diggers," Hazard remarked.

"No," Carson agreed, "it doesn't. But we've got plenty of dynamite;

one or two good blasts will fix it."

He went back around the cliff dweller's hut and called to his workmen.

"Bring up two cases of dynamite, and fuses and caps!" he shouted.

Looking down, Hazard saw Gunnar Drugge stop work on the tent he was erecting and trot over to the truck that carried the dynamite. Before the other workmen had hardly understood the words, Drugge was on his way up the path at a dog-trot, a case of dynamite on each shoulder.

"Whatever we may suspect of that guy," Carson remarked, "he certainly is a model workman."

The Scandinavian was breathing easily as he reached the top of the trail in spite of the fact that he had made the ascent at a half run.

"Here you are, sir," he said.

Carson motioned him to follow, and Drugge did so. In front of the great rock slab, he lowered the boxes gently to the ground.

"We want to plant the dynamite around that slab and blow it out," Carson said. "I think that's the entrance to the cave."

Without the slightest change of expression, Gunnar Drugge nodded and began opening sticks of dynamite, setting caps into them.

"Where do you expect to set off the blast, sir?"

"We'll hook all the sticks up to a fuse that's long enough, so well have time to get down safely before she goes off," Carson answered.

Jerry Hazard, who knew little about the secrets of dynamiting, stood off at one side, his eyes glued on Gunnar Drugge. But the more he watched the Scandinavian work, the more certain he was that he was merely a faithful employee. Drugge and Carson had placed half the sticks of dynamite around the edge of the slab when Gunnar stopped, lighted a cigarette.

"Isn't that dangerous while you're working with dynamite?" Hazard asked.

Drugge looked up with a grin. "I've done it many times," he said, "but if it makes you nervous, sir, I won't."

Without even waiting for Hazard to answer, he took the newly-lighted cigarette out of his mouth and snapped it over the edge of the cliff shelf. A moment later, he got up.

"I'm afraid I didn't bring enough fuse," he said. "I'll go down and get more."

Carson glanced about.

"Yes," he agreed, "you'd better get more. I'll finish packing the sticks."

Drugge started down on a run. Hazard watched him until he was out of sight, far down the trail. Suddenly, his body grew rigid as though seized by a swift, freezing convulsion. His wide-eyed stare was held by a thin wisp of smoke drifting up from behind the stone slab.

That smoke couldn't have been from the cigarette Drugge had lighted because he had tossed it over the edge of the cliff.

Hazard let out a wild yell of alarm, "Carson! Look out! Run!" He leaped forward, grabbed the astonished Carson by the arm and almost pulled him off his balance as he jerked him to his feet.

"What the—" Carson demanded.

"Smoke!" Hazard yelled. "It's coming from behind the rock. A fuse has been set off! Come on!"

They were already running headlong down the trail. Down, down they raced without saying a word. They were putting all their effort in an attempt to escape from a horrible death. They reached the place where the trail steepened and doubled back under the shelf of rock where the watcher's house stood.

Hazard was thinking with lightning speed, trying to figure what would happen when that blast came. He grasped Carson's coat as they reached the corner and pulled him back.

"Over here!" he yelled indicating the carved-out opening where the watcher's house stood.

They had barely crouched at the back of the ledge when a gigantic roar sounded in their ears. The enormous rock wall against which they taken refuge shuddered. Huge rocks flew out over the shelf where the watcher's adobe hut had stood—but the building was no longer there. It had been transformed in the smallest fraction of a second to a great cloud of dust and flying particles of adobe that swept out over the wide valley from the mountainside.

"Look!" Carson yelled. "The slab's gone! There's the opening of Suicide Tomb!"

"Yes," Hazard snapped, "but how about that Scandinavian devil who tried to trap us up there?"

"Never mind him," Carson gasped eagerly. "The blast is over and the tomb is open. Come on!"

Hazard followed the archaeologist in a dead run up the path. They climbed over the piles of debris that had been left by the blast and raced on. Carson was already inside when Hazard reached the entrance. The young archaeologist was staring at something on the floor. It was white and still. He turned to Hazard excitedly.

"White bats!" he exploded. "Look at them. And I'll bet they're alive. They were probably only stunned by the force of the explosion."

"White bats!" Hazard gasped. "I never heard of them."

"Nor I," Carson said enthusiastically. He picked up the one nearest him; it was limp and lifeless. "We've got to have some of these," he said. "But first, I want to get a look at the cave. Don't you get an enormous kick, Hazard, out of being the first human to walk into a tomb after it had been closed up for thousands of years?"

"Yes," Hazard said, trying to follow Carson as he plunged deeper into the blackness. "Particularly when there's a strange legend connected with it. Boy, what a newspaper story this will make!"

It was as dark as pitch in the great cavern. The only light filtered from the opening in the cliff face. In this uncertain luminance, the cave was revealed as circular in shape. Suddenly a light flashed on in Carson's hand. He uttered a loud exclamation of astonishment.

HAZARD ran forward through the darkness. He noticed as he went that the floor was as smooth as though it had been cleverly laid by expert workmen. Probably it was a solid, smooth slab of stone that thousands of years before had settled away from what was now the domed roof.

He saw other white shapes lying on the floor and guessed they were more white bats. But he didn't take particular notice of them, for his attention was drawn to Carson, who was flashing the beam of his electric torch on what looked like a great heap of bones.

As his eyes became more accustomed to the light, he saw something strange about these bones. They glowed with a weird, purplish light. But even so, he wondered at the reason for Carson's sudden exclamation. Certainly they had expected to find skeletons here.

"Do you see anything strange about those skeletons?" Carson asked quickly.

"Of course," Hazard replied.

"They give off a phosphorescent light."

"No, no," Carson answered a trifle irritably. "Anything underground as long as they've been and subject to certain chemical action is apt to become phosphorescent. What I'm referring to is the way these skeletons are placed. Don't you see anything funny about that, Jerry?"

Now Jerry Hazard looked at the masses of bones more closely. Instantly he realized what Carson meant.

"Don't you see that there aren't any skeletons in the center of the tomb?" Carson went on. To emphasize the fact, he swept the center of the great open space with the beam of his flashlight.

"That's right," Jerry admitted in an awed voice. "The whole center of the cave is clear."

"Not only that," Carson said, "but look at the way the skeletons are lying around the edge of it. All the same. Their heads toward the wall."

"Yes," Hazard nodded, "and they're almost evenly spaced, too."

"They are about as evenly spaced as they could be. And it's easy to see why. At a rough guess, I should say that there are nearly four hundred skeletons. Stay here a minute, Jerry. I want to try something."

Rod Carson vanished into the thick darkness. Hazard surveyed the dim interior of the cavern. He saw that it was perfectly round. With its high, vaulted ceiling and smooth, stone floor, it reminded him of a cathedral without seats or altar. An eerie feeling crept over him as he fancied that the place was filled with the four hundred odd ghosts of these dead people. He listened intently as he heard Carson's hollow footsteps stride from the door of the tomb, straight across the center to the opposite side. He was taking long steps about a yard in length with a measured tread; evidently he was pacing off distance. Instinctively, the newspaper man counted those paces.

"Forty-four, forty-five, forty-six," he finished as Carson reached the opposite wall. "I made it forty-six paces," he said to Carson as the other came back to where he stood.

"I made it forty-seven," Carson said. "Either one's near enough."

"But what was the idea?" Hazard asked.

"Well," Carson explained, "in either case, the space is about one hundred and forty feet in diameter which makes nearly eight hundred feet in circumference to this amphitheater of death. You notice that the skeletons are placed about two feet apart. Allowing two feet of space to each skeleton gives us close to four hundred bodies—just as I guessed."

"I can't figure out," Hazard said as he stepped closer and examined the skeletons, "how these bodies came to be placed at such regular intervals."

"I'd appreciate it a lot if you would tell me," Carson said. "It's one of the strangest things I have ever seen in my life. Do you suppose it was a religious rite?"

"That's a thought," Hazard said. "Put yourself in the place of one of these plague-ridden prisoners. Here you are, sealed up in this tomb, your comrades dying off one at a time—"

"Wait," Carson broke in, "there must be some place for air to get in. Otherwise these white bats wouldn't be able to live in here."

"Doubtless," Hazard nodded, "through crevices up in the top."

"All of which comes back to my theory. These people didn't die of suffocation, but of the plague. Now suppose we were trapped in here with several hundred others. What would we do with the bodies of the dead ones? We wouldn't want to leave them where we'd be stumbling over their rotting carcasses; so we would either pile them in the middle and finish the rest of our plague-tortured lives around the edge, or we would drag them to the edge and continue to live in the middle."

"Not a bad idea," Carson commended. "I think that last theory is a closer guess than the first. We would prefer to live in the center because the ceiling is higher and the air would be fresher."

As Carson spoke, Hazard was bending down over one of the skeletons. All membranes and cartilage that had held the bones together had rotted away long ago and the bones lay where they had dropped. Hence, there was a pile of ribs, sections of back bone, and leg and arm bones all laid out flat on the stone floor of the tomb, in the general shape of the dead human's body as it had fallen. The legs had been bent up at the hips and knees. The arm bones were left in such a fashion as to indicate that the body had dropped on them when it fell; for they could be seen through the mass of ribs which lay on top of them.

Carson inspected this gruesome mess grimly.

"What I'm wondering about," be ventured, "is what happened to the last survivor? Who laid him out in the space left for him?"

"That's a thought," Hazard said. He stopped suddenly as the light from Carson's electric torch fell full upon the skull of the skeleton under discussion. His eyes narrowed; for the skull had been crushed so hard that it had fallen apart in four sections.

Breathlessly, Hazard jerked his head toward the skeleton lying on the other side. Carson's beam obediently shone down on it. The two men stared in petrified astonishment.

"It looks, Carson," Hazard said, when he found his voice, "as though we've got to alter our theory a little."

"Wait a minute," Carson suggested. "Let's check up on this." He rose quickly and began moving down the narrow lane left between the heads of the skeletons and the outer wall of the cave. Slowly, he progressed around the circle, shining his flash light from one skull to another.

A weird supernatural feeling grew in Jerry Hazard as he followed at Carson's heels around that gruesome aisle. In the light from the electric torch he could see that every skull had been crushed in. In some cases the skull was merely cracked at the top; in others the broken portions had fallen away after the flesh had rotted from the bone structure.

Not a word was spoken as they rounded that horrible circle of separate masses of spidery, purplish bones. Hazard was counting them as they moved along.

"Three hundred and ninety-six," he said as they reached the entrance, "if my count is right."

"It is," Carson confirmed. "I checked them too. I can't figure out why this cave was named the Suicide Tomb, Jerry. These are murders. These people were all struck on the head and then dragged over to the wall and dropped in a circular formation around the edge of the tomb."

"You mean," Hazard said, "that someone came in here, killed them one by one, dragged them to the side, and then left."

"Not necessarily," Carson countered. "I didn't say that the murderer left. He might have been an executioner sent up here with the group."

"And then," Hazard suggested, "after he had knocked them all over the head and placed them so neatly in a circle, he went over to the only space that was left and hit himself over the head?"

"Well, yes," Carson said a little defiantly. "You can't say that's impossible."

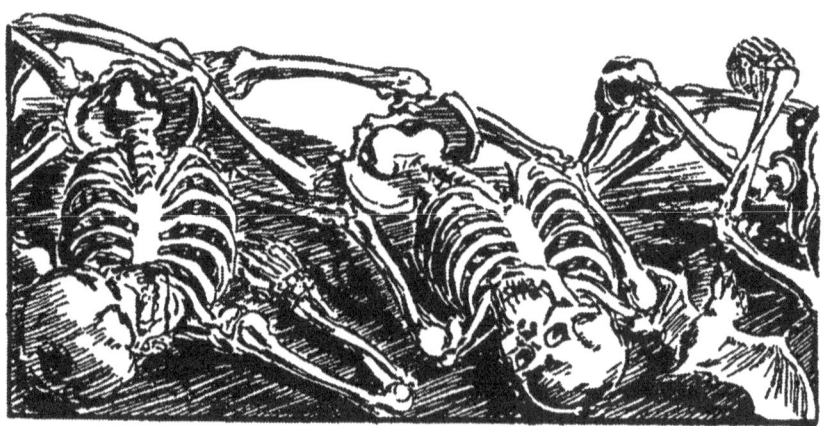

"All right," Hazard said. "Can I borrow your light a minute."

He took the flash from Carson and walked across the center of the great cavern, sweeping the floor with the yellow ray.

"I was looking for the instrument used to bash in the brains of these poor prisoners," he explained after several moments search. "But there isn't a loose rock or a wooden dob or anything of the land. Of course, there are some small rocks by the entrance, but those were loosened in all probability by the explosion."

CHAPTER FIVE

The Purple Star

CARSON'S words were cut off by the sound of a voice calling from the entrance to the tomb–an Oriental, high-pitched voice. "Mr. Clarson! Mr. Clarson! You all light?"

"Come on," Carson said in sudden relief. "We're okay. That's Ah Yung, my cook, and that must be my crew behind him. They've come up to find but why we didn't return after the explosion. Maybe they've got some news of Drugge." Then Carson raised his voice again. "Come in. Ah Yung. We're all right. Have you seen anything of that blond devil that brought up the dynamite?"

They met Ah Yung at the entrance; he was grinning with joy.

"You all light, Mr. Clarson," he said happily. "That velly good. We all velly happy."

"Have you seen anything of Gunnar Drugge?" Carson repeated.

A rangy Westerner by the name of Lahey, who was foreman of the crew, spoke up.

"No," he said. "We ain't seen nothing of him. We reckoned he was up here with you, Mr. Carson."

"Well, if you find him," Carson instructed, "shoot him on sight. He nearly got us. He deliberately lit a fuse and set off a premature explosion."

"We ain't seen nothing of him," Lahey repeated; the others confirmed his words with negative shakes of their heads.

"I don't imagine we'll see anything of him, either," Carson ventured, "if he has anything to say about it. Come in here, you fellows. There's something I want to take down with me tonight. Ever hear of white bats?"

The workmen gaped. Then Lahey said, "White bats! I don't reckon I ever heard of such a thing."

"Neither did I," Carson admitted, "but this place is full of them. They're lying on the floor, stunned by the explosion. I want you fellows to go in and pick up a half dozen of them. We'll put them in a cage. They're about the rarest thing I've struck yet. But watch them carefully. They'll be regaining consciousness any minute now, and their bite might be poisonous.

"Yes, sir."

"Lahey," Carson continued, "you go down to camp as quickly as possible and empty one of the packing cases. Cover it up with wire or slats—anything that will keep these bats in. There's one over there. You can see how big it is. Have the cage ready when we get down."

"Yes, sir." Lahey nodded and started off down the trail, his boots clanking hollowly on the stone path.

The rest of the crew went gingerly inside the cave. Evidently, they didn't find this place much to their liking. However, a few minutes later, they came out again, each carrying two white bats, wrapped up in their shirts so they wouldn't be able to bite.

Lahey had the cage ready when they reached camp. One by one the men deposited the strange white captives in the improvised cage. A Mexican held the last two, which were returning to consciousness. They struggled weakly as he shoved them toward the box. He skillfully maneuvered the first one in while Lahey held a slat loose; but he fumbled the next one and darted back as it snapped at him.

There was a flutter of wings and the white beast rose in the air. Lahey uttered a loud curse and clamped the slat over the opening but it was too late.

Jerry Hazard drew his gun. He lost the bat for a moment in the darkness. An instant later it was charging down with folded wings. He uttered a cry of warning. "Look out! Here it comes! It's trying to get one of us!"

He aimed his automatic and pulled the trigger.

Blam! Blam!

But the bat kept on coming. Carson's revolver was out, too, and he was also shooting.

Bam!

The bat's wings flicked out instinctively. Hazard ducked and raised his hands to ward it off, but the bat swerved with lightning speed and turned away. There was a low, smacking sound. Then they saw the Westerner, Lahey, fighting the bat away from his face. He uttered a cry of pain, and then a curse as he struck vainly at the white beast.

"Bite me, will you, you little so-and-so," Lahey bellowed angrily. "I'll show you."

He knocked the bat to the ground with a powerful blow and reached forward quickly, grasping the stunned animal by the body. With a quick movement, he removed the slat again and dropped the bat into the cage.

"There, you varmint," he said as he slammed the slat back in place,

"stay in there where you belong."

Then the husky Westerner turned to the others. Apparently, he was completely unconcerned about the whole affair. But not so with Carson and Hazard.

"Where did he bite you?" Hazard asked.

"Oh, it wasn't nothing," Lahey shrugged. "He nipped me on the forehead. At least I thought he bit me, but maybe it was just his claws digging into me when he tried to light and hold on."

"Come on over here, Lahey," Carson urged, taking him by the arm. "I want to look at that forehead."

"Oh, it ain't nothing to worry about," Lahey remonstrated. "I've been bitten by worse things than that and lived."

But Carson had him under the light now; both he and Hazard were staring at the Westerner's leathery forehead.

"Where was it—" Carson started to ask; but he stopped short as Lahey pointed to the center of his forehead, above the bridge of his nose.

There were five tiny marks there, none of them more than an inch away from the rest. They were in a perfect circle, equally spaced and curved inward toward the center. They were purple in color.

"Look!" Carson explained. "It's spreading!"

Lahey's forehead wrinkled in a frown.

"Spreading?" he asked. "Say, you fellows aren't fooling with me, are you? I don't feel anything on my forehead. Why, it ain't even swollen," he said.

"You're sure you don't feel anything at all, Lahey?" Carson asked.

The Westerner felt the place tenderly.

"Well," he admitted, "maybe it does feel a little numb, like when you strike your funnybone. What's it look like?"

Carson took a small mirror out of his pocket.

"Take a look at it yourself."

Lahey took the metal mirror and tipped his head down.

"Why, ain't that funny," he said half to himself. "The place where the doggoned bat bit me looks like a star."

"It is," Hazard said. " A five-pointed, purple star."

The Westerner's face looked a little worried now as he said, "Wh-what does it mean?"

"I don't know," Carson admitted. "Let's hope it doesn't mean anything."

Suddenly Lahey turned away from the light.

"Hey, where are you going?" Hazard called out.

"I got an idea that I want to try out," the Westerner said. "Maybe I'm right and then again maybe I ain't, but I reckon I'm going to find out soon."

Carson and Hazard followed him back to the packing case where they had imprisoned the bats. Lahey picked up a lighted lantern near the cage, shook it vigorously before the slatted opening. After a moment he cried out triumphantly.

"There, that's the idea I got. And it felt like it, too, when the little varmint bit me."

One of the bats was straining to get at Lahey. The mouth of the white beast was protruding through two of the slats, its jaws opened and closed, again and again, as it snapped savagely at the light.

"See that?" Lahey asked as he pointed excitedly to the teeth. "It's got five teeth, three on the upper jaw and two on the lower and they're pointed back. The middle tooth on the upper jaw is a little farther ahead than the other two. When the little varmint bites into a man's flesh, the teeth go in like the five points of a star. There must be something on those teeth that turns the flesh purple."

"Yes," Carson nodded quickly. "It's probably the same chemical substance that turns the skeletons purple."

Lahey jumped as though he had been shot.

"Huh?" he demanded. "What's that about purple skeletons?"

"Yes," Carson said. "There's almost four hundred skeletons in that tomb where you found us. And their bones are purple."

Lahey straightened like a nan who was suddenly condemned to die. His voice was quite steady as he said, "You reckon, then, I'm going to die of the same plague that killed them four hundred people?"

"No," Hazard denied instantly. There was no need of worrying Lahey. "No, I don't believe that. It seems reasonable to expect that after thousands of years the plague would have died out."

"But them bats," Lahey insisted. "They might carry the bugs."

"I doubt it," Carson said. "Come, into my tent and I'll give you a shot of something that will guard against infection."

They entered Carson's tent and the young archaeologist got out his medicine chest. He filled a hypodermic needle from a small bottle, bared Lahey's arm, and forced the liquid under the skin.

"Something like a rattlesnake dope that they give you after you've been bitten, ain't it?" the Westerner ventured.

"Something on that order," Carson admitted. "Now take the rest of the night off. Go to your tent, roll up in a blanket and get a good sweat. I think you'll be all right in the morning."

"Sure," Lahey grinned. "I guess so. Don't worry about me. I'll be all right. Good night."

When he was out of earshot, Carson and Hazard faced each other.

"You know," Hazard said, "that was a clever idea Lahey had."

"You mean about the plague being carried by the bats?" Carson queried.

"Yes," Hazard nodded. "It is possible."

"It's one of the weirdest things I have ever seen," Carson remarked. "That five-pointed purple star on Lahey's forehead looks as though the man was marked by the hand of death."

"If he is," Hazard ventured, "how about the rest of us?"

"That's not a particularly nice thought to turn in on," Carson shrugged.

"I'll say it isn't," Hazard agreed. "But I've got work to do."

HAZARD brought out his portable typewriter and set it up on a folding table in the tent he and Carson occupied. He slipped a piece of paper into the typewriter and began writing. In a few minutes he was engrossed in an account of the Suicide Tomb. He was dimly aware of Carson working at another folding desk, making notes and sketches. Sheet after sheet of type-written manuscript left Hazard's typewriter as the hours wore on.

"I guess I'll take a little walk around and see that everything is okay," Carson said when he had finished his work.

"Right," Hazard said, nodding absently. Then, as an afterthought, "Better go well armed."

"I will," Carson assured him.

Minutes later, Jerry Hazard finished his story, sealed it into an envelope that was already stamped with the name and address of his syndicate, and laid it on the table.

Confused thoughts surged through his tired brain as he leaned back in his canvas-backed folding chair—thoughts of the Suicide Tomb, white bats, Wu Fang, Lahey and the purple star. And in the background of all those thoughts was the vision of Mohra. He could see her before him as he reached for a cigarette and his lighter.

He placed the cigarette between his lips and started to raise the lighter toward it. But the flame never touched the tip.

"Hazard! Hazard!"

It was Carson's voice. Hazard leaped up, dashed out of the tent. Just outside he bumped into Carson so forcibly that both of them were nearly knocked off balance. The young archaeologist grabbed his arm and pointed up to the cliff.

Jerry Hazard stared with bulging eyes at the entrance to Suicide Tomb. A great ball of fire glowed thru, like a huge lavender frosted bulb.

"For the love of heaven, what is it?" Hazard breathed.

"It's dying down now. It was much brighter when I first called to you."

As Carson finished speaking, the glow went out. There was an instant of total darkness and then a white shape appeared against the great mass of stone. Giant wings stretched out in the darkness.

"It's a bat!" Carson cried. "A giant bat!"

"No, it isn't," Hazard countered excitedly, "it's just a shapeless cloud of something."

Without realizing it, Carson and Hazard had been striding toward the trail that led up to the base of the cliff. Clumps of sage rose ominously in the pitch darkness about them, but their attention was fixed unwaveringly on the phantom shape above.

"I never believed in ghosts before," Carson muttered, half to himself, "but I could almost be sold on the idea now."

"Yes," Hazard cut in, "but don't be too sure. Remember—"

The newspaper man stopped short as a low cry from the camp behind them reached their ears. This was followed by a loud shout. It sounded like Lahey's voice.

They turned quickly and raced down the path toward the camp, but the voice of the Westerner had died away before they reached it. The rest of the men in the crew were plunging toward Lahey's tent.

"Somebody light a lantern!" Carson shouted. "Lahey's in trouble."

They dived into the dark tent that Lahey shared with another member of the crew. In the light of a lantern that one of the Mexicans held up they saw that one of the two cots was empty. On the other lay Lahey's partner, a stubby little Westerner known only as 'Shorty.'

His breath came with a horrible rasping sound; there was a gaping wound in his chest. His eyelids fluttered as Hazard bent over him.

His lips quivered and in a voice that gurgled with the blood from his injuries, he gasped. "Stop it. It got—Lahey."

"It?" Hazard demanded. "What got Lahey?"

The man's chest heaved spasmodically, then one word came rushing out in a mass of blood: "Gorilla."

Hazard stiffened at the mention of that word. Carson, he was aware, had whirled round to face him.

"Gorilla. For the love of Heaven, Jerry. There *is* a gorilla behind it all. The track outside the window. And now—"

Hazard was bending over the bloody form of Shorty. The man had gone limp after uttering that one word. Hazard's hand went under the bloody shirt. It was hard work controlling himself while he probed in the red, sticky mass of life liquid.

With a sigh of relief, he drew out his hand and wiped it on the blanket.

"Shorty needn't worry any longer," he said huskily.

With that, Carson spun round, as though he had been waiting for confirmation of Shorty's death, and dived for the flap of the tent.

At the same instant a cry came from a Mexican outside.

"*Sacre Dieu!* The ghost! It come! It kill us. Run, run, *señors!*"

Hazard was on Carson's heels. He plunged out into the darkness of night, staring about frantically. His gun was ready.

Then, there in the open, before the tent, he stopped and his eyes seemed about to leave their sockets.

Coming down from the entrance of Suicide Cave was the white phantom. It was settling lower and lower over the camp. Settling with the motion of a great monster, phantom cat, creeping up, ready to spring.

Carson, in a panic of desperation, was raising his automatic.

Blam! Blam! Blam!

The gun barked again and again. But the white shape came slowly, inexorably on.

CHAPTER SIX

Chinatown

A WEEK before, Jerry Hazard and Val Kildare had parted company in New York. As they spent that last evening together in the Press Club, Hazard had voiced his reluctance to go.

"It seems that I'm leaving everything behind when I go out to Arizona on that assignment," he remarked.

A smile crossed the face of the government man who was reclining in an easy chair, one long leg wrapped around the other. He puffed luxuriously at his long panatella cigar.

"I know, Jerry, old man," he said. "It must be tough to pull up stakes and leave the part of the country where a certain beautiful girl is located. But cheer up. It's only a short assignment. In the meantime, I'm going to spend every minute trying to locate Wu Fang and Mohra."

"You are sure they're—" Hazard began.

"I am very much afraid that Wu Fang is alive," Kildare said, forestalling the newspaperman's question. "And, of course, Mohra too. I hope when you get back, I'll have Wu Fang's hiding place ferreted out so that you and I can write the closing act to his career."

Jerry Hazard glanced at his watch and rose.

"Well, here's wishing us both luck," he said, rising. "Want to accompany me to the train?"

"Sure."

THEY STOPPED in at his newspaper office on the way to the station. On the way out, Hazard spotted his friend, Cappy, and called a greeting. The newsboy looked up at him eagerly.

"Listen, Jerry," he said. "I hear you're going out to Arizona to hunt skeletons. How's chances of my coming along in your suitcase?"

Hazard laughed and patted the boy on the shoulder.

"You can't spend too much time away from that paper route," he said. "What's going to happen to that college education you're working for?"

"Yeah, I know," Cappy argued, "but then maybe you'll need a good scrapper."

"He's the one who will need protection," Hazard said, jerking his head toward Kildare. "He's staying here and—" Hazard lowered his voice confidentially— "you can bet that if Wu Fang is in Chinatown, Kildare is going to locate him."

"Gee," Cappy exclaimed, "I guess I'd better stay here. Don't you worry, Jerry, I'll keep an eye on Mr. Kildare."

VAL KILDARE lost no time in carrying out his plans. He took up quarters on the edge of Chinatown, and after enlisting the help of the police of the Mulberry street station, began a thorough search for the Dragon Lord of Crime.

He interviewed numerous Chinese. Some had been in the toils of the law at one time or another; others were reputable merchants and importers. But always he made the same challenge: "We are going to trap Wu Fang and we will pay plenty of money for any information leading to his capture or death. What do you know?"

The usual answer was an eloquent shrug of Chinese shoulders and a placid, "I know nothing of Wu Fang."

On the night of Mrs. Marshall's brutal murder, Kildare put his question to one of the most powerful men in Chinatown. Wong Chu had never been questioned by the police in connection with any crime. To Americans, he was known as a high ranking mandarin, termed *kwan* by the Orientals. Kildare had added him to his list of prospects because Wong Chu was a member of the same secret order, the Chang Li, to which Wu Fang belonged.

Wong Chu's house was dull and drab like the other dirty two- and three-story buildings that lined the narrow, twisting streets of Chinatown. But when Val Kildare announced himself, he was ushered into a gorgeously-appointed interior. Priceless hangings, rare pieces of statuary, and incredibly beautiful Oriental rugs all blended into a general effect of tasteful magnificence.

He knew very well that he might be walking into a trap. It was possible that Wong Chu was in direct league with the yellow fiend, in which case death was an absolute certainty for Kildare. Two minutes passed while Kildare stood in that great hall, guarded by a giant Chinese servant. Then a muffled gong sounded from somewhere in the interior. Again and again the gong sounded. Three muffled, wide-separated beats.

As though that third beat had been a signal, the servant bowed stiffly from the waist. "You will follow, please, honorable sir," he said.

He led the way to the rear of the hall and through a wide door. Here he stopped, and in a voice strangely high pitched for one of his huge size, he sang out:

"Announcing the presence of honorable Mr. Kildare."

Kildare advanced. He found himself in a large square room. The decorations were Oriental. But the furniture, with the exception of a few pieces of teakwood, were occidental, evidently purchased from the best American furniture houses. A strange combination, nicely blended in good taste.

Walls were hung with the finest of tapestries, heavily embroidered. Light filtered through the room from round lanterns placed on carved wood pedestals. Kildare's feet sunk deep in the silken nap of a powder blue Chinese rug.

In a carved, ebony, straight backed chair, a slightly built Chinaman sat. He rose to his feet. He was quite short, but there was a distinct bearing of importance about him. He smiled and walked toward Kildare.

"I have heard much of you, Mr. Kildare," he said, "but this is our first meeting. I am honored. You will sit down?"

"Thank you." Kildare nodded. "You are Wong Chu?"

The Chinaman nodded. He was alert, almost nervous in his actions. When Kildare had sat down, he clapped his hands. A large Chinese entered, bearing a heavily inlaid tray of tea apparatus and cakes that he deposited on a round stand.

"You will have tea?" Wong Chu asked as he began to pour.

The government man thought quickly. It would be easy for Wong Chu to dope him with the tea; but he had little choice. He was alone in this great house; although he had his gun, what chance would he have against Wong Chu and his flock of servants, men who would, beyond a doubt, die at the slightest command from their master?

He nodded quickly. "Thank you, yes," he said pleasantly. He was soon glad of this decision, for although he had had occasion to drink a considerable amount of tea in the past few days, this was the best he had ever tasted.

They had sipped half the contents of their cups before Kildare came to the purpose of his call.

"I presume you know my business, Mr. Wong," he said.

Wong smiled. "You are a government man," he observed.

"Yes," Kildare said with a nod, "and in that capacity I have made it my business to trail one of your race by the name of Wu Fang."

Wong Chu nodded his head very slowly without speaking.

"I thought perhaps you might know where Wu Fang could be found," Kildare said. "I can assure you that the United States government will pay well for information leading to his arrest."

There was a moment of awkward silence while Wong Chu looked intently at Kildare. Then he spoke.

"May I inquire why you ask me this question, Mr. Kildare?" he asked politely.

Kildare leaned farther back in his chair and wound his right leg around his left. The time had come and he was ready to shoot the works.

"Because, Mr. Wong," he said imperturbably, "I have been led to understand that you are a member of the Chang Li."

The face of Wong Chu never changed; his eyes never wavered from Kildare's gaze. After a moment, he answered.

"You have been correctly informed, Mr. Kildare," he said. "I am a member of the Chang Li. The gentleman of whom you speak, namely Wu Fang, is also a member of our secret order. Or perhaps I should change that statement and say that he was a member. I do not know his present standing with the order. In speaking like this, I am violating one of the rules of our association. You understand, of course, that I have spoken in the strictest of confidence."

"You may rest assured, Mr. Wong," Kildare said, "that the confidence will not be broken. Do you know where Wu Fang is at the present time?"

Wong Chu looked thoughtful for a moment; then he smiled calmly.

"No. At the present time I do not know where Wu Fang is."

"Do you know the location of his hideout here in Chinatown?" Kildare probed.

The smile still lingered faintly on the Oriental's face.

"Mr. Kildare, as you doubtless know, yourself, Wu Fang is a very mysterious individual. It is indeed quite difficult to follow his movements."

"In other words," Kildare observed, "it is useless for me to question you any longer, Mr. Wong."

"Your assumption is correct," Wong Chu bowed. "However, permit me to make this one fact clear to you, Mr. Kildare. I have nothing in common with Wu Fang except the fact that we are both members of the secret order of Chang Li. You may rest assured that I am in no way connected with him. Regardless of what you may hear to the contrary, I am a law-abiding citizen."

Kildare finished his tea and stood up.

"I believe I understand your position more clearly now than I did when I came," the government man said as he extended his hand. "Thank you for being frank with me and also for a most delicious cup of tea."

Wong Chu rose and bowed.

"The meeting has been a pleasure, I assure you," he said politely. He clapped his hands, and the giant servant who had admitted Kildare appeared almost as though by magic. The government man was ushered into the spacious hall and out into the night.

He shrugged his shoulders disgustedly as he walked down the sidewalk. He had played his trump card and lost. He was quite sure from Wong Chu's conversation that Wu Fang was still in Chinatown, but he was as much in the dark as ever concerning the yellow devil's whereabouts.

He glanced up and down the narrow, dark street, wondering what to do next. A Chinese shuffled down the opposite sidewalk. Another came up and passed him, apparently taking no notice of him. Nevertheless, the government man watched him until he passed out of sight around the corner. Then Kildare turned aimlessly and followed in the same direction. He was trying to figure out some move that would give him the secret of Wu Fang's hiding place.

He had gone perhaps twenty paces down the street when he realized he was being followed.

Placing his hand on his gun, he grasped the butt and strode on faster. Twice he turned and glanced back—but there was only darkness behind.

It wasn't until he reached the corner that he heard a definite sound—the pad of running bare feet. He whirled. A figure crouched some ten feet away. An arm raised—something was hurtling toward him. Instinctively he ducked to avoid the expected knife; but even as he did so he realized it was not a knife.

"Stop, or I'll shoot!" he ordered. He whipped out his automatic—but the yellow man had vanished. Vanished in the pitch blackness.

He lunged, scooped up the object that had been thrown at him. It was a wadded paper. Then he charged toward the shadows where the Chinese had disappeared. But there was only a stairway leading down from the sidewalk, blocked by a solid, locked door at the bottom. There were two other doors leading into the building. But they, too, were securely fastened.

CHAPTER SEVEN
The Place of Angels

THAT creature following him had been clever, but not clever enough. The third time Kildare turned he hadn't been quick enough to hide; and so had tossed the message which it was his mission to deliver.

There was no use trying to hunt him any longer. He had apparently vanished into thin air; so Kildare strode down the sidewalk toward the corner where a dim light burned. Perhaps the message was from Wong Chu to let him know where Wu Fang was. He stopped beneath the light and carefully unfolded the crumpled ball of paper. There were two lines scrawled in a childlike hand writing.

"You may find Wu Fang at the Place of Angels."

Kildare repeated the last three words over again to himself. A smile creased his lips. The idea of Wu Fang in the Place of Angels was ludicrous.

"That's a good one," he chuckled. Place of Angels? The phrase sounded familiar.

He turned abruptly and walked back down the street toward the Mulberry street police station. He spread the note out on the desk before the captain.

"What do you think of that?" he asked.

The captain glanced over the note; his brow furrowed in thought. "That's funny," he said. "Wu Fang in the Place of Angels!" He laughed heartily. "Somebody must be kidding you, Kildare."

"Perhaps," Kildare insisted, "but I've got a hunch it's a hot tip. Isn't there a dive called the Place of Angels?"

A patrolman who was lounging on a bench got up and came over. "I think I know of a place by that name," he said. "It's down on the East River front. Wharf rats and foreign seamen hang out there. It's a tough place."

"Any Chinese?" Kildare demanded.

"Yeah," the officer nodded. "You'll find some of them there now and then."

"But what's the idea of naming it the Place of Angels?"

The cop chuckled. "When I first saw it, I thought it was a mission; but it seems that the guy who runs it is a Spaniard, Portuguese or something of the sort and his name is Angel. Some down and out artist who used to frequent the joint painted the sign for nothing. He left out the apostrophe between the 'l' and the 's'."

"Where is it?" Kildare asked.

The cop led him over to a big map on the opposite wall and pointed out the location.

"But if I was you," he went on, "I'd take the riot squad with me if I was going down to that joint."

"Thanks," Kildare said, "but I'm not going down to raid the place. I just want to look around."

"Even at that," the patrolman argued, "the riot squad wouldn't be a bad thing to have along."

Kildare smiled, shook his head. A riot squad was the one thing he didn't want. If Wu Fang were at this dump, a riot squad would surely scare him away.

A HALF hour later, he reached his destination. The street was dark as pitch where he left the cab, and it seemed to him as the vehicle moved away, that he had never been so alone. Except for a light two blocks away, the entire street was shrouded in murky gloom. The smell of the sea and the stink of the docks hung about the place. On the river-side of the street, great wharves loomed like menacing giants in the night. From inside a squat, two-story frame building came the whine of music and the beating of a set of drums.

Now, two swaggering forms came swinging down the sidewalk. Without hesitation or notice of Kildare, they barged into the place, the doors swinging easily before them. Almost immediately the doors burst open again, and a boisterous drunken seaman came sailing out under the expert propulsion of a two-hundred-and-fifty-pound bouncer. He landed in the gutter at Kildare's feet. He picked himself up with difficulty, clinging to Kildare for support.

As he regained his balance, he took hold of the lapels of Kildare's coat, and in a marked German accent, he asked, "You have got money, *mein freund?* You will take me in and buy me one more drink, *ja?*"

Already the man's breath reeked like the dump end of a distillery.

"No, you've had enough already," Kildare said. "But I'll give you a half dollar if you'll tell me some things about that place you were just thrown out of."

He produced a fifty cent piece and held it before the bleary-eyed seaman.

"Here's your half dollar," he said. "Now tell me, are there any Chinamen in there?"

"Shinamen?" the man hiccoughed. "Shinamen? Maybe one or two. I don't know. But there's a girl who dances."

Kildare's eyes narrowed as he snapped, "Girl?" With that, he took hold of the man's arm and shook him slightly as he asked, "What kind of a girl? Is she white or is she Chinese?"

The other giggled foolishly. "*Jawohl*, she is Chinese all right," he said. "She is such a little thing, *Und Ach du Lieber* can she dance! But she looks so innocent; she is little more than a baby, *mein freund.*"

"A Chinese girl?" Kildare repeated. "Is she with any Chinamen?"

"*Ach nein*," the drunk shrugged. "I didn't see her with any Chinamen. Angel, he brings her out and introduces her himself. She has been a special attraction for two nights now. I have spent all my money so that I could watch her dance. A month's pay, *mein freund*, in two days."

"Okay," Kildare nodded. "Here's your half dollar. Don't come back in here to buy a drink if that's what you're going to spend it for."

"*Ach du Lieber*," the German groaned, "I get kicked out of Angel's place because I haven't any money to buy more liquor and therefore I cannot stay to watch the girl dance. Just one more dance I should see. This half dollar will buy two drinks and I will see the Chinese girl again—"

"You heard what I said," Kildare interrupted sternly. "Get moving down the street."

The seaman staggered back and nodded. "*Jawohl, jawohl*," he said.

Kildare watched him until he merged into the shadows; then he turned abruptly to the door and entered. The place was gray with smoke and the low ceiling held it down close. Kildare guessed at first glance that there were twenty-five tables ranged very close to each other with three or four chairs at each. In the center of the room, before the bar, there was a small empty space left for dancing. Two grinning colored boys furnished the music, as they worked feverishly over a piano and a set of drums. Nearly every table was filled, but Kildare saw an empty space at the long bar that ran along the opposite side of the room from the door.

A dozen or more dock hands and freighter seamen were dancing with some frowsy females, jostling each other in the small space as they kept time to the fast rhythm.

Kildare caught the bouncer giving him a hard look. He shifted his eyes immediately and let them play about the room over the various sev-

enty-odd occupants at the tables and bar. He spotted two Chinese sitting at a table well off the dance floor and noticed, at the same time, the eyes of one were full upon him.

The government man threaded his way toward the empty space he had seen at the bar. He ordered a whiskey-and-soda and proceeded to sip it leisurely.

Now he turned and swept the room with his eyes. Something strange was going on in the corner where he had seen the two Chinamen. One of them was still there, but the one who had stared at Kildare was gone.

Kildare had noticed a sleek little man, apparently Spanish or Mexican, standing at the other end of the bar. He decided that in all probability this was Angel himself. Now the man moved out to the dance floor and was greeted by a burst of wild applause and raucous shouting. He held up his hands for silence.

"One minute, *señors*," he cried, "One minute. We will now have another dance by the beautiful Chinese girl. Nee-Sa will do for you the dance of the flapping sails."

With that announcement, the place went wild with shouting and applause. The piano struck up a slow, rhythmic tune while the trap drummer dropped his sticks and substituted a clarinet. A small, lithe figure glided into the bright light before the goggle-eyed seamen. In spite of Val Kildare's usual composure, he started suddenly at first sight of the girl. She was an Oriental, there could be no doubt of that. Her youthful, innocent face was belated by the more mature curves of her lovely body. Her eyes were exceptionally large for a Chinese girl and held a look of childish trustfulness. She was extremely graceful, Kildare noted, as she continued her dance. Twice she turned and looked full into his face; but she also did that to the other men standing with their backs to the bar as well.

A drunken seaman next to Kildare turned to slap him on the shoulder but missed; throwing open his coat instead and displaying the badge inside. However, Kildare apparently didn't notice it. He was too engrossed in the dance.

"Ain't she a honey?" he leered vulgarly.

Kildare nodded and pulled his coat together again, keeping his eyes constantly on the girl. A few moments later, she ended her dance, to the wild roar of applause. The girl leaped up and cried out something as her eyes ranged over the faces of the drunkards nearest her. Kildare heard her call, "I want a drink. I will choose the man who will buy me a drink."

Her eyes swept down the bar and came to rest on Kildare's face.

"This man will buy me a drink," she said and planted herself beside him along the bar.

Kildare sensed something out of the ordinary in the move the girl had made. Either he was being trapped, or she had chosen him for a special reason.

She spoke now, low and soft, like the eager voice of a child, "I will have champagne."

Kildare obligingly paid for her drink while the little Chinese girl sipped it luxuriously. He felt her edging closer to him, as though she wanted protection.

"You are a policeman," she said, glancing at his face. "I am being kept here against my will. I was sold to this man Angel by Wu Fang."

Val Kildare tried to hide his astonishment at what the girl was saying. This baby-faced girl sold to this Latin devil by Wu Fang!

The girl lifted her glass high, spinning around with her back to the bar, crying out in her childish voice, "I drink a toast to all of you big, strong men."

There was another round of applause from the rowdy customers, as they crowded around her.

"There is a door behind you that opens out into the alley," she said to Kildare, under cover of the clamor, "if you are to save me, you must take me out through that. It is locked, and Angel has the key. But it's not very strong and I think you can push it open. Do so and I will follow you at once."

Kildare gave a short nod. A moment later, he turned his head and studied the door that she had mentioned. It was quite flimsy and one good lunge with his shoulder ought to push it open easily.

"You know Wu Fang's hiding place?" he asked.

"Yes," the Chinese girl whispered. "I was going to tell you. If you will get me out of here, I will take you to—"

A look from Kildare silenced her. The girl's back had been turned to the men farther down the bar, but now as she turned, she saw that Angel was coming down behind the bar toward them.

The thing would have to be done now, if at all, Kildare decided.

He placed little faith in the girl; but no risk would be too great if it opened a new avenue of procedure. Perhaps, in his cunning, Wu Fang would outdo himself.

"Follow me," he hissed quickly under his breath. Then he whirled around and hurled himself at the door.

Blam!

The door shuddered but still held. A cry of warning went up and Kildare, although he wasn't looking in that direction, knew that it came from the lips of the man called Angel.

"*Sacre dio!* Stop or I will kill you!"

Kildare sprang back, ducked low, and hurled his body at that door again. As his shoulder struck the door, a dagger thudded quivering into the wood near his head. Next moment, the door gave way and Kildare plunged into the night. He had hold of the girl's wrist and dragged her after him.

A shot rang out from inside the Place of Angels. Shouting and cursing. It was pitch dark out there in the alley; and the sudden change from the brightly lighted room to the inky blackness blinded Kildare.

CHAPTER EIGHT

Yellow Trap

VAL KILDARE'S left hand was still clutching the girl's wrist, but now it was she who was leading the way through the darkness.

"This way," she said.

As he followed her, Kildare's eyes grew more accustomed to the darkness, and he could see that they had taken a jog in the narrow alley to the right. Nee-Sa swung him left again, and when they did that, he could see a street light far ahead.

The mob was still pursuing them. A bullet whistled over their heads. When they reached the light, Kildare saw it was on a back street. Not a taxi was in sight; except for one or two wavering drunks, the thoroughfare was deserted. He pulled Nee-Sa into a shadowy doorway and crouched there, gun in hand. But, strangely enough, the sounds of pursuit had died away. After a few moments Kildare stepped out and looked around. The street was quiet.

"Come on," he said. "We seem to have given them the slip."

They walked six blocks before reaching a main street. Kildare waved a taxi to the curb. He pushed Nee-Sa inside and climbed in beside her.

"Chinatown," Kildare told the driver. Then he turned to Nee-Sa. "Is that right?"

There was a muffled, "Yes," from the girl who was huddled in one corner of the cab.

"Okay," Kildare told the driver. "I'll give the address later."

He pulled shut the window and turned to the Chinese girl once more.

"Your name is Nee-Sa?" he asked.

"Yes, sir," she said with a pathetic little nod.

"All right. You say that Wu Fang sold you to this bird Angel?"

"Yes, sir," the girl repeated. "That was almost a week ago. He sold me to Angel as one of his own possessions. Since then, I have been kept in a barred room with an ugly old woman to guard me. I wasn't allowed to go anywhere; the only times they let me out was when Angel wanted me to dance at intervals all night long."

"And you know where Wu Fang is?" Kildare asked.

"I will show you his hiding place in Chinatown," the girl said.

"But look here," Kildare protested. "You say he sold you to Angel nearly a week ago. How do you know that he is still in town?"

"I have seen him since then," the girl replied. "He came twice to the Place of Angels to see me dance."

Kildare studied her through thoughtful eyes.

"Where is Wu Fang to be found?"

She smiled; her eyes were wide and innocent.

"His underground room is reached through a staircase that leads down out of an alley between Bayard and Pell Streets. I cannot tell you the number, but I will tell the driver where to stop."

Nee-Sa kept her word. She directed the driver to a narrow alley, hung in a pall of ominous gloom.

An early morning fog was beginning to settle over the city, hiding objects that should have been clearly visible even in the darkness of night. Kildare and the girl got out. He dismissed the taxi and surveyed the dark interior of the alley.

It looked strange and forboding; rifts of gathering mist drifted slowly through it, forming ghostly shapes. Kildare was sure he saw a gray figure move out of a door on one side of the alley into a niche on the other. His jaw set grimly.

Nee-Sa took his arm. "Come with me," she said softly.

There were no lights in either of the squalid buildings that flanked the narrow passage. In fact, there were no lights anywhere. He slipped the safety catch off his automatic and tightened his fingers on the trigger.

Suddenly, he felt the girl stop; she opened a door. A faint, musty, Oriental odor met his nostrils.

"Follow me," she said softly.

They moved slowly down a steep stairs. Again the girl whispered, "Please do not make a light. If I am caught doing this, Wu Fang will surely kill me."

As they reached the bottom of the stairs, Kildare paused to listen. Impatiently the girl tugged at his arm. He followed her. It was a dismal, damp underground passage, as still as a tomb. Kildare tried to walk on tiptoe, but in spite of his best efforts, his footsteps were quite audible. Suddenly he realized that he was at the top of another flight of stairs.

A strange sensation crept over him—a premonition of another presence beside Nee-Sa and himself. Yet he could hear nothing. Suddenly Nee-Sa stopped and although Kildare couldn't see anything, he sensed that the corridor had come to an end.

"Here," the girl whispered close to him, "is where I must leave you. This door ahead opens directly into his private room. If he discovers that I have escaped and have led you here, I will surely be killed."

She drew his hand forward; he felt the knob of the door.

"There," she said. "Is your gun ready?"

"Yes," Kildare whispered back.

"Then let me get behind you before you open the door."

He hesitated, then flattened himself against the wall so that the girl could pass.

"I wish you much luck," she said softly. "I hope you succeed in killing Wu Fang. I will wait a moment to see you burst open the door."

"Thanks for bringing me here," Kildare whispered. "Keep back out of the way now. I'm going in."

THE index finger of his right hand was pressed against the trigger of his automatic as he turned the knob quickly with his left hand and pushed open the door with a sudden forward thrust of his body. He found himself standing in a dimly-lighted chamber. But there were no luxurious Oriental rugs, no tapestries. The room was bare. So it was a trap after all.

As he half turned to face the girl, suddenly he felt a sharp pain as of a needle jabbing through his back. Instantly his arms became numb and lifeless, and likewise his legs. He could feel the numbing force coursing through his veins as his heart pumped it; but his ears, eyes, and brain were still active.

He heard his gun clatter to the floor as it slipped from his nerveless fingers; out of the corner of his eye he caught sight of Nee-Sa easing him down as he fell—although he couldn't feel her hands upon his shoulders. His entire oody was seized by the numbness now; he had no sense of feeling whatsoever.

The girl was laughing like a happy child.

"So, Mr. Kildare," she chuckled delightedly, "you thought I was a poor little girl who had been sold in slavery. You did not know that I am one of Wu Fang's cleverest agents and that you had been turned over to me to get rid of. I am doing this on my own way. You see, I am clever like Wu Fang, and I can think of many interesting ways to kill people. Wu is not even here. He has left Chinatown."

Kildare listened helplessly as the girl babbled on.

"I brought you here even more easily than I had expected. I was afraid I would have to stick you with the needle before this. I hope you are quite comfortable now."

She stepped a little distance from him and surveyed him. Kildare stared back at her. He had walked into a death trap—but even now he could no other way. It was his duty to follow down every clue—no matter how dangerous.

The girl left the room and he heard her running swiftly down the corridor.

"Do not worry," she called to him, laughing. "I will be right back. I am not going to leave you lying there until the narcotic wears off."

A few moments later, she returned carrying a small wooden box about a foot square. She tipped it up so that he could look through the wire mesh which covered the top.

There were three beasts in there—beasts be had seen before. They were the lizard-rats that gnawed into the vitals of the stomach and spread their poison inside, causing awful torture. The three little beasts clawed and scratched the wire in an effort to escape.

"You will soon have your fun." Nee-Sa laughed gaily. "Look, Mr. Kildare. I will place the box on the floor three feet away from you. Three feet away from your stomach. Now I will open your vest and shirt so that they may get at you more easily after they have gnawed their way out of the box."

The girl bent over him and did as she had said. Then from somewhere in her clothing, she took out a small vial and held it up before the light.

"You see this tiny bottle?" she asked. "It contains a liquid whose odor is very attractive to my little friends. They will do anything to get at it. Now you see—" As she spoke, she poured some of the liquid on her hands and rubbed it around the outside of the cage. "—it makes them eager to escape."

There was an immediate scramble inside the box as the little beasts struggled to get out. Next, Nee-Sa turned to Kildare, poured more of the liquid on her fingers and rubbed it over his stomach.

"Now I believe you are ready for death," she laughed cheerfully. "I will put out the light so that you may enjoy the sound of the little beasts gnawing. Perhaps you think that the narcotic will protect you from the pain of their attack and you will die without torture. But do not deceive yourself. I have timed my performance well, and the effect of the narcotic will wear off just enough so that you will still feel the pain and yet you will not be able to get up."

With a ripple of gay, girlish laughter, Nee-Sa turned and stepped toward the door. The light went out.

"When you are in hell, never trust a woman," she advised as she slammed the door.

Then all was still except for that horrible gnawing sound as the three vicious little beasts fought to escape from their prison. Their teeth were working desperately, insanely, to get at the strange liquid.

Kildare struggled desperately to move but the narcotic held him helpless.

Scrape! Scrape!

But in spite of that continuous gnawing, his nerves remained calm. He knew that it was possible to fight off a drug by working hard enough; so he struggled with all his might and main to move his arms and legs.

THE gnawing continued endlessly. *Scrape! Scrape!* Perspiration rolled out on his forehead in giant beads as he struggled to make his drugged muscles obey the command of his brain. A surge of sudden joy came to him as he realized that he could feel a prickling sensation in his legs and arms. But an appalling realization came to him that more than counteracted his joy. If the numbness was leaving him, it probably meant that the lizard beasts would soon escape. Any moment now, they might rush across that short intervening space and attack his vitals before he could regain strength enough to get up and fight them off.

The gnawing sounded more hollow now. Kildare was positive that his end was only a matter of minutes away—but he kept struggling.

Then he heard a voice from the door, a boy's voice.

"Mr. Kildare! Mr. Kildare! Are you all right?"

It was Cappy! Kildare tried to shout out in answer but the only sound that came from his throat was a husky, rasping mumble. Cappy pounded on the door. He was turning the latch but the door was locked. Then Kildare heard the boy fling himself against the panel again and again. It bulged under his onslaught but held.

Scrape! Scrape!

The animals were nearly out of their box now. The sound of splintering wood came to Kildare as he tried to mumble an answer to Cappy.

"Try again," he gasped.

Blam!

The boy's body hit the door again. Kildare's struggles were helping him to shake off the affect of that drug. Prickles of feeling were returning to his arms and legs. He was crawling to his knees. His knowledge of drugs and their action was going to save him—if he could move fast enough.

Up on one knee. Straining every bit of will power. Up and groping along the wall now for the switch.

Bam!

Again Cappy hit that door. This time the portal blasted inward. At the same instant Kildare's hand found the light switch; a dim light filled the room.

The first of the beasts was out of the box. The others were crowding through the hole. Cappy leaped and came down with both feet, crushing it. Kildare was trying to help him stomp the beast to death, but his movements were yet too slow.

Cappy crashed down on another, then stopped to pick up Kildare's gun from the floor. The only remaining beast was leaping at Cappy. The boy darted back as Kildare managed to kick with his right leg. The animal was caught squarely and hurled against the back wall of the room. It lay still.

"Gee," Cappy panted, "I'm glad I went down to headquarters to see you. They told me where you'd gone so I went to the Place of Angels, too; and I saw you coming out on the back street with the Chinese girl. But gee, Mr. Kildare, you didn't need me. You were almost out of the jam by the time I got in."

The two turned down the corridor through the smashed door.

"I might have been lost without you, Cappy," Kildare assured him kindly. "Remember, I was half doped when you entered. I'm afraid that first beast would have gotten me before I could move fast enough."

AT Lafayette Avenue they took a cab for police headquarters. A yellow envelope was handed to Kildare there. He tore it open, read it.

"Here's something that will interest you, Cappy," he said. "A telegram from Jerry Hazard in Tombstone, Arizona. I know now why Wu Fang isn't in Chinatown. He and his agents are out there. We're leaving as soon as we can catch a westbound plane!"

CHAPTER NINE
Plague of Death

KILDARE'S guess concerning Wu Fang was correct. The yellow Dragon Lord of Crime was ensconced with his agents in the largest of the ancient pueblo cliff dwellings overlooking the valley where Hazard and Carson were encamped.

Those ancient dwellings had been built hundreds of years ago to protect their occupants. The great rooms on the lower floor had no windows or doors. Entrance was effected by ladders which led down from the second floor.

Strange, portable lights of Wu Fang's own invention lit the pueblo in a weird fashion, casting long, ghostly shadows.

Wu Fang paced slowly back and forth in the largest of a series of rock chambers. Now and then his narrow, slanted eyes glanced at the door on the left, and again, up at a hole in the ceiling.

At the creaking of a ladder, he turned expectantly.

"It is time for him to return," he breathed softly. "He has been gone for over an hour."

The door opened; a giant gorilla stood there. The beast came in, bent with a burden on its back. It carried the body of a white man and a cage of white bats. The yellow fiend pointed to a cot on one side of the room.

Without a sound, the gorilla padded across the room, bent down, deposited the lanky form of his captive on the cot, set the bat cage on the floor, and stood up. Then the beast did a peculiar thing. He lifted the gorilla head from his shoulders, displaying blond hair and a face that was distinctly Scandinavian.

Wu Fang smiled: "You have done well, Gunnar."

Gunnar Drugge bowed. "Thank you, Master. I would have had trouble capturing Lahey if it had not been for that clever trick of the ball of fire at the mouth of the cave and the ghost that rose from it."

"I thought that would attract their attention sufficiently," Wu Fang said. "You have amply compensated for your failure to kill Mr. Hazard and Mr. Kildare. Now I will begin tests. You may go, Gunnar."

When Drugge had departed, Wu Fang walked over to the recumbent white man and studied the purple mask on his forehead intently. Then he clapped his hands and a yellow servant appeared.

"Bring me the book entitled *Ancient Plagues*!" Wu Fang commanded.

The servant bowed and a moment later was back with a large, black book. Wu Fang moved nearer to the light, oblivious to the fact that the eyes of the white man were following every move he made. He studied that book for a long time. Finally he closed it with a snap. A frown wrinkled his high forehead.

From a small medicine case that stood on an improvised table, he took out a splint that was about three inches long and tapered to a needlelike point. Next, he took a tiny bottle of milky white liquid from his case. He walked leisurely over to the prisoner and smiled down at him.

"How does it feel to be an experiment?" he asked. "You cannot answer, but a slight application of this preparation will loosen your tongue."

He held the small bottle to the light, uncorked it, and dipped the bamboo splint into it. Quickly, he removed the splint and with a skilled gesture pierced the flesh of Lahey's throat. He replaced the cork in the bottle and tossed the splint into a corner of the room. Turning, he put the bottle back into its place in the medicine case.

The Westerner was mumbling. A moment later, his voice came out strong and coherent again, and a curse broke from his lips.

"What the Hell's the idea?" he demanded hoarsely.

Wu Fang told him with a fiendish smile: "I saw the bat bite you on the forehead, and I see now that there is a five-pointed purple star where it attacked."

"If you think I'm going to give you any information, you yellow rat," Lahey rasped, "you're crazy!"

Wu Fang chuckled with amusement. Suddenly, the calm confidence of the Oriental seemed to frighten Lahey. The anger left his face abruptly and his weather-beaten skin turned ashen.

"Wh-what are you going to do, kill me?" he asked.

"This experiment, I trust, will end your days in a most horrible death," Wu Fang said calmly. "But if you live through it, you shall have your freedom—perhaps. You are to answer some questions now. What was your sensation shortly after the bat attacked you?"

"I—I think my forehead felt sort of numb," Lahey stammered.

Wu Fang nodded. "Then the poison is going through your system."

"The poison!" Lahey cried. "You mean from that bat's teeth?"

"Yes," Wu Fang nodded slowly, "from the bat's teeth. I believe that the mark on your forehead is a curse. It means that after a certain period you will die. We will have to wait and see."

He bent over the helpless Lahey, lifted the man's eyelids, and peered up at the top of his eyeballs. Then he studied again the purple star on his forehead for some minutes.

"Yes," he said when he had finished his inspection, "we will watch the development as it takes place and see what the reaction will be." He turned slowly. "The Suicide Tomb, the Suicide Tomb," he muttered. "That's a peculiar name for a place like the cave of the purple skeletons. Gunnar says that the bones are lying in a circle around the wall." He turned back suddenly to Lahey. "Have you been inside the Suicide Tomb?" he demanded.

Lahey nodded.

"Did you see the skeletons?"

"Some of them."

"They are purple?" Wu Fang asked.

"The bones that I saw were," Lahey admitted.

"Did you see the skulls with holes in them?"

"No."

Wu Fang mused thoughtfully, "White bats." He stared down at the half dozen bats in the cage near him. "They are beautiful little creatures. They will make a fine addition to my farm for hybrid breeding."

He smiled suavely, then clapped his hands. A yellow servant entered.

"Send Gunnar here at once," he ordered.

WHEN the Scandinavian was before him, he said, "There are some questions, Gunnar, that I wish to ask you concerning the skeletons in the cave."

Drugge bowed. "What is that you wish to know, Master?"

"I have been wondering," Wu Fang said, "if there was any evidence of how these skulls were crushed. You know, of course, that the skull is divided into four parts. There is a line of division running from the forehead straight back through the middle and there is another line where the skull is knit together running across the top of the head."

Again Gunnar Drugge nodded, "Yes, Master."

"Were the holes at the back of the skull or near the top where the four quarters come together?"

"They were at the top," Gunnar assured him.

"All of them?" Wu Fang persisted.

"Yes, Master."

"That is good. Now we come to the next point. Would you say that these skulls were crushed from an impact on top or that they had been broken from inside—as though a small dynamite explosion had occurred?"

Gunnar Drugge looked at him in bewilderment.

"I don't understand what you mean, Master," he said. "How could a skull be blown apart by dynamite? Besides, those skeletons have been there for hundreds of years. They were there long before anyone knew anything about dynamite."

"True," Wu Fang admitted. "I didn't mean that dynamite was the direct cause of the eruption; I used that merely as an example."

For a long moment Drugge hesitated in deep thought. Then he said, "I'm quite positive that the skulls were cracked from a blow on the outside. The broken bones had not fallen out of some of the skulls and they remained dented. Those that had separated had fallen inward."

"That does not help any," Wu Fang snapped. "That is all, Gunnar. You may go."

Wu Fang sat frowning after Drugge left. His eyes shifted slowly from the figure of Lahey on the cot, to the cage of white bats.

"That is strange," he said aloud. "In the history of pestilence there is a description of one disease among the ancient peoples of South America which manifested itself in a brain fever that created such enormous pressure inside the skull that sometimes the brain splits open. South America is not so far from Mexico and Mexico is just across the border from here. I was in hopes that I had discovered the solution for the broken skulls—but I was mistaken. I will have to make other tests." He turned to Lahey. "How do you feel now?"

"About the same," Lahey said.

"You have no trace of a headache?"

Lahey's face went white. "Yes," he said, "You're enough to give anyone a headache."

Wu Fang's eyes glinted with sudden fury; then a smile of sardonic amusement creased his lips. For a moment he stared at Lahey, then he clapped his hands.

"Send Tanya to me," he ordered when the servant appeared.

In less than ten minutes, a girl entered. She was tall and blond; she moved with unusual grace and was indescribably beautiful. Her clear blue eyes focused on Wu Fang, wide and appealing.

"Ah, Tanya, my beautiful blue-eyed one," Wu Fang smiled, "never have I seen you appear so lovely."

"Thank you, Master," she answered. Her voice was clear and soft.

"I have work for you, Tanya," Wu Fang said. "I am sending you with Mohra to the camp below this cliff. Two young men are down there. It will be your task to bring them up here. Say nothing of what I tell you to Mohra. The orders which she will receive, you will hear me tell her. Remember that at all costs, the two young men must be brought where my agents can seize them. I need them for some experiments I wish to perform."

The girl nodded obediently, "I will do as you wish, Master."

"I see you have a handkerchief in your hand. Let me have it, please."

Tanya gave the lace handkerchief that she held to Wu Fang. The yellow fiend took a small bottle from his medicine case. Holding it well away from him, he touched the open mouth to the handkerchief and tipped the bottle up several times. Then he tossed it to the floor.

"Let it lie there for a moment," he said. "The liquid which I put on it will give off a delicate perfume but do not trust it. One whiff of it will render a person unconscious. It is a hundred times stronger than ether, but unless the handkerchief is directly in front of the nostrils, it will not harm you. Carry this handkerchief with you. It is to be used only in an emergency."

"And what am I to do?" the girl asked.

"At the proper time you will suggest that Mr. Carson and Mr. Hazard come up here and try to capture me. You will offer to show them the secret path that leads to this great shelf on the cliff."

Tanya's eyes widened.

"Do you mean, Master, that we are to show them your hiding place?"

Wu Fang nodded. "Yes, my blue-eyed one, that is my plan."

"But perhaps they will do you harm."

"Do not fear for me," Wu Fang said. "I will be prepared. From the moment you reach the camp a number of my agents will be close to you. If the two gentlemen refuse to come with you wave your handkerchief before Mr. Carson's nose. He will fall unconscious and when Mr. Hazard bends over him, do the same with him. Then scream for help. That will be the signal for my agents. But do not use the scented handkerchief unless absolutely necessary; for it will delay my experiment if I have to bring them to consciousness first."

The girl nodded. "I understand."

"Then go and fetch Mohra," Wu Fang said. "There is no time to waste."

Tanya left. A few minutes later, she returned with the lovely, dark-eyed Mohra. Wu Fang smiled benevolently on both of them.

"My children," he said, "I have made a decision. As you doubtless know, there is a camp below us at the bottom of the cliff. You, Mohra, will be particularly interested to hear about it. Your lover, Mr. Hazard, is there with a friend of his, a Mr. Carson. I have realized that I can not hold you any longer; when love calls, there can be no barrier strong enough to resist it. And since it would not be fair, Mohra, my lovely one, to release you without freeing Tanya also, I am sending you both away—you to Hazard and Tanya to do as she likes."

Mohra didn't seem to be under Wu Fang's spell any longer. Her eyes suddenly sparkled with a new joy of living and her face lighted up with hope and anticipation.

"You are doing this for me—for us?" she burst out suddenly. "You—"

"Do not wait to thank me." Wu Fang smiled. "You must go while I am in the mood to let you. I will send one of my agents to guide you down the trail to the bottom of the cliff."

Mohra's eyes were misty, and she turned quickly away to hide the tears of happiness that welled up in them. Tanya looked back at Wu Fang as she followed Mohra out; and she saw that his green eyes were no longer smiling but were glowing brilliantly with that brutal look of command that she knew so well.

CHAPTER TEN
Death Bait

AS THEY dashed out of the tent after the Mexicans' warning cries, Jerry Hazard and Rod Carson saw the white phantom, which had seemed to be settling down over the valley, slowly rising again.

Once again it moved toward them. Hazard's muscles grew taut as he stared up at that phantomlike thing. Suddenly the darkness around their camp took on an aspect of terror and menace. The giant cliff before them didn't seem part of this earth, but assumed a strange shape in the gloom of night.

Then, as the ghostly phantom began to rise once more, he frowned.

"Do you realize what this is?" he demanded. "The whole thing is a plant. A trap to call everybody's attention away from the camp! We've been tricked! Our attention was drawn by those strange sights away from the real danger down here. Gunnar Drugge is one of Wu Fang's agents. The yellow fiend wanted Lahey for his experiments to see what effect the bite of the white bat would have on him."

The newspaper man's voice broke off as the spectral shape that had hovered about the cliff suddenly vanished.

"Did you see where it went?" Carson cried.

"No," Hazard flashed back, "and probably nobody else did. It's my guess that Wu Fang is in the cave. He was probably very close to us when we were there. But if that's true, I don't see why he didn't trap us then."

When they returned to the tent a few moments later, Carson yawned.

"For my part," he ventured, "I'm going to turn in."

"All right," Hazard agreed. "You turn in and I'll stay up and watch. Somebody has got to keep his eyes open for the rest of the night or we'll never see dawn."

"No," Carson said, shaking his head. "I'm not going to let you sit up all night to guard my camp, Jerry."

Hazard laughed, and again there was a tinge of nervousness in his voice.

"Don't worry," he said. "It isn't your camp that I'm guarding. I'm sitting up to save my own life. Anyway, I wouldn't be able to sleep if I did turn in. I'll tell you what well do. You curl up on the bunk and I'll sit on a chair and turn the light out. Order everybody in the camp to quiet down and make no noise. Then if I hear any sounds, I'll know that something is up."

Carson gave the order to his men and then, without removing his clothing, dropped down on the bunk. Hazard turned out the lantern and waited in the pitch blackness for something to happen. He took out his automatic, removed the safety catch. Minutes passed—an hour—two hours. Dawn would be breaking shortly.

Carson's rhythmic breathing soothed Hazard's tired brain, robbing him of his alertness. Suddenly, he heard a sound. It came like a short gasp or a choked-off sob, and he thought it was accompanied by a series of running footsteps. He sat bolt upright in his chair and clutched his automatic. A nervous tension gripped him; he was ready to shoot at the first move.

The sound came again. He was sure now that he heard running feet. Cautiously, he got up from his chair and stood taut and motionless. And as he stood there he heard a girl's voice.

"Jerry! Jerry! Jerry!"

It was Mohra's voice! The newspaper man was stunned. But he was aware of a great joy surging over him. Mohra was free! She was coming to him! This would spell the end of her captivity, under the fiendish influence of Wu Fang. For as long as there, was a breath in his body, Jerry Hazard would not let her get back into the clutches of the yellow devil.

He darted out of the tent.

"Mohra, here I am!" he called.

"What's up? What's going on?" Rod Carson demanded.

Out of the murky night, Hazard saw two shadowy figures running headlong toward him. The first was Mohra. He cracked out a command to the second figure, "Stop or I'll shoot!"

Mohra stumbled, half exhausted. Hazard caught her with his left arm.

"No, no, Jerry! Don't shoot!" Mohra gasped. "That's Tanya! She came down here with me."

Hazard released pressure on the trigger of his gun and tightened his arms around Mohra. He entirely forgot Rod Carson, who was plunging out of the tent, and the person whom Mohra had called Tanya—in fact, ge forgot everybody and everything in the world except the fact that he held Mohra, the girl he loved so desperately, in his arms. He was kissing her again and again and she was responding willingly, eagerly.

Time stood still. Hazard had no idea how long he and Mohra had been standing like that until Rod Carson's amused voice broke in on his ecstasy.

"Well, what is this—a party?"

"It's all right, Mohra," Hazard assured her, seeing her surprise. Turning to Carson, he said: "You remember my telling you about the beautiful girl who was held to that devil Wu Fang by some strange power? Well, this is she. Mohra, this is my friend, Rod Carson."

Carson bowed. Mohra, still breathless, introduced Tanya to the two men. The blond beauty, unlike Mohra, seemed perfectly calm. Hazard began asking hurried questions. She answered them clearly and coolly.

"How did you get out west?" Carson demanded.

"We were brought here," Tanya told him, "by Wu Fang."

Hazard nodded. "But how did you escape?"

"Well, you see—" Mohra began.

But before she could go on with her explanation, Tanya broke in with: "We partially escaped and then on the other hand, you could truthfully say we were permitted to go free."

"Permitted to go free!" Hazard exploded. He looked from Mohra to Tanya and back to Mohra again. "I don't get this at all," he said. "I can't picture Wu Fang letting you go, Mohra. Are you being followed by his agents?"

Mohra shook her head. "No, Jerry. We were guided down here by two of them, but they have gone back now. I am beginning to think that Wu Fang is not as bad as—"

"Wait," Hazard interrupted her. "You'll have my brain spinning with more of this. If you're not being followed by Wu Fang's agents, it will be safe for us to go into our tent and put on a light. I want to get this straight."

He motioned the two girls inside the tent. Carson lit the lantern, and offered their guests the only two chairs.

"Suppose, Mohra," Hazard suggested, "that you start at the beginning and tell us all about it. In the first place, how did you get out here in Arizona? Tanya says Wu Fang brought you. Is that right?"

"Yes." Mohra nodded. "I imagine that we flew most of the way. I don't know for sure as I was in a partly dormant state during the entire journey."

"In a casket, no doubt," Hazard ventured, shuddering at the thought.

"I imagine so," Mohra said.

Carson was staring at them in utter amazement.

"A casket?" he repeated incredulously. "You mean you were brought out here from the East in a casket?"

"Wu Fang has transported us from one place to another in many strange ways," Mohra said.

"It's quite comfortable," Tanya assured him. "You see, we don't know anything that happens from the time we are put under the influence of the drug until we awaken."

"All right, Mohra. Go on, please," Hazard begged.

"I don't remember just how long ago it was that we arrived here," she said.

Carson turned to the beautiful blue-eyed Tanya, "Did you come out the same way?" he asked.

The girl nodded, "So far as I know."

"But I should think there would be a great deal of danger in that sort of thing," Carson ventured.

Tanya bestowed a bewilderingly lovely smile on the young archaeologist. "When one is forced to work with Wu Fang, there is always danger."

"And you are compelled to work with him?" Carson demanded.

"Yes, we were," Tanya told him.

"Up to less than an hour ago," Mohra added. "Tanya came to my room then and told me that Wu Fang wanted to see us both. When we went before him, he told us that he was giving us our liberty and sending us down here to your camp."

Tanya said: "Wu Fang and his agents are established up there in one of the main dwellings on the large cliff. You can see it from here when it is light."

Carson and Hazard exchanged significant glances.

"I think that explains a lot of things," Carson ventured. "From up there he can watch everything we do down here. Why, he must have even seen Lahey bitten by the white bat."

"Who is Lahey?" Mohra asked.

"He's a long, lanky Westerner," Hazard told her, "who was bitten by one of the white bats that we captured in the cave."

"Yes." Mohra nodded quickly. "I know now who you mean. He is with Wu Fang now."

"Good Lord!" Carson exploded, "What are they going to do with him?"

"Wu Fang," said Tanya, "is planning to use him as an experiment."

"Lahey?" Carson exploded. "Why, that yellow devil, I'll—"

Hazard raised his hand.

"Wait a minute, Carson." He turned to the blond girl, "What do you know about this, Tanya? You seem to have been with Wu Fang more than Mohra."

"I have," the girl admitted. "You see, I don't think Wu Fang trusts Mohra as much as he used to, because of her—her feeling toward you."

"But what is he after?" Carson demanded.

"In the first place," Tanya continued, "Wu Fang is always searching for something that will enable him to control the world. If he can discover the secret of this ancient plague, if he can learn how to control it, he can demand concessions from every country in the world under threat of releasing this horrible disease."

Carson turned to Hazard.

"Jerry," he said, "I didn't believe that any human could be as bad as you said Wu Fang is. But now—"

Hazard looked grimly amused.

"I know exactly how you feel," he said "I felt the same way about it myself when I first heard of him, but I've seen too much of his work to doubt anything that I hear now."

"But Lahey!" Carson cried. "We've got to get him out of this. We can't stand by while he's used as a human guinea pig. Tanya, can you show us the way back to Wu Fang?"

Tanya hesitated. "I think so," she said at last. "But Wu Fang is leaving shortly."

"Just a minute," Hazard protested "We have others to think of beside Lahey. Mohra—and Tanya have just escaped Wu Fang. Is it fair to lead them back?"

Hazard realized they might be stepping into a trap. He trusted Mohra. But this girl—this beautiful blond creature—he wasn't so sure of her. On the other hand, Wu Fang must be captured or killed at all costs, trap or no trap. And they had no time to lose. There never was where Wu Fang was involved.

"I am sure," Tanya said, breaking the silence, "that I would be willing to take that chance. I would do anything to see Wu Fang get what he deserves."

Mohra frowned at her reproachfully.

"Do you think, Tanya," she asked, "that Wu Fang deserves such hatred? Remember, he let us go out of the kindness of his heart."

"I doubt," Tanya countered, "whether Wu Fang ever had a kind thought in his life. I have an idea that he let us go because he no longer had need of us. Don't let this one thing make you forget all the beatings he gave you."

"I guess you're right," Mohra agreed after a moment's thought.

"And if that isn't enough," Tanya continued, "remember what he's trying to do now. Think of humanity, of what will happen if he releases this plague. He has no pity for anyone. Why should we pity him?"

Mohra nodded. "You're right. We must go. We must make sure that Wu Fang's reign of horror and crime is finished. Jerry, we will show you the secret path back to the main ledge."

THERE were seven altogether in the party that started across the plain through the night. It was pitch dark, the hour just before dawn. Hazard, Carson, and the two girls moved ahead while the three Mexicans who had accompanied them brought up the rear.

Tanya and Mohra found it more difficult to locate that secret trail than they had at first imagined; but finally they found it and the party started the ascent to the main cliff.

They were nearly at the edge of the cliff on which had been built the Indian dwellings of hundreds of years ago, when Hazard stopped short and turned quickly to Carson.

"I don't hear the Mexicans behind us," he said.

Carson spun around; they searched the darkness frantically.

"Pedro! Manuel! Carlos!" Carson called softly. There was no answer. Hazard grew rigid, clutched the butt of his automatic tighter.

"All the way up, Carson," he whispered hoarsely. "I had the feeling that we were being followed by somebody. Now I'm sure of it. I'd be willing to bet my life that if we went down along the trail again, we'd find the three Mexicans lying where they fell."

"I can't believe it," Carson protested "I didn't hear any sound. Certainly there were no shots."

"With Wu Fang," Hazard told him, "there are never any shots and there is seldom any sound to warn of danger."

"But how—"

"Wu Fang has various methods of getting people out of the way," Hazard said, "A poison dart, some little beast crawling up the body of the chosen victim, a snake hanging from a rock at the side of the path."

"But why," Carson demanded, "would he do that to the three Mexicans and not to us?"

Hazard's voice was very low and tense now as he said, "He's saving as for later. Come on, Carson. We've gone this far, and we can't turn back now."

Mohra and Tanya listened intently to the two men's conversation, but said nothing. Silently, they turned and moved on toward the top of the trail behind Carson and Hazard.

Suddenly, they found that it was no longer dark; they could see objects quite clearly. They were on a point where the trail levelled on to the ledge. Brush grew in the cracks of the ridge, rooted in earth from the rimrock a quarter of a mile above, washed down through generations of storms. To the left, the cliff dropped off into sheer space. Over the tops of the brush and small trees were visible the two- and three-story ancient adobe buildings that covered the wide ledge.

Hazard heard a rustle at his right in the brush. He spun around. Without taking time to aim, he shot once in the direction from which the sound had come. There was a scream of pain. A half-naked body leaped into the air and then sank from sight in the brush again.

As though that had been a signal, a head appeared over the edge of the trail. A yellow slant-eyed wicked face. The owner of that face lifted a small, bamboo blowpipe to his lips.

"Look out!" Hazard yelled to Carson. "There, behind you!"

Hazard spun around. His automatic barked twice. The first bullet entered the face of the yellow agent.

Hazard pulled Mohra up beside him.

"Come on," he gasped. He charged through the thicket. He heard a choked cry from Carson and spun around. The young archaeologist was falling. Tanya was climbing to him.

Then came a crashing sound from behind. A figure leaped, clutching at him with powerful hands. Hazard's right arm went limp. His gun was wrenched from his fingers.

Mohra was battling with another figure, beating him with clenched fists. Then the girl darted back with astonishing speed. Realizing that she couldn't cope with the enormous strength of her assailant, she fled from him.

Jerry Hazard went down on his face, though in the frenzy of fight he realized with a feeling of horror that Mohra was running straight for the edge of the cliff!

Twice the half-naked brown-skinned attacker lunged forward and clutched at the girl. He missed her each time. She flung a look over her shoulder and came within two strides of the brink of the precipice. Hazard caught the depth of expression—love, pleading, desperation—in those lovely, dark eyes as they met his. Then she turned and ran on.

Hazard was trying desperately to cry out for her to stop, but his breath had been knocked out of him, and he couldn't utter a sound. Mohra took one more step to the edge of the cliff. Then she hurled into space. Her agonized screams echoed up through the canyon.

CHAPTER ELEVEN

Lair of the Dragon

WITH the horrible realization that Mohra had gone, Jerry Hazard was possessed of sudden, insane strength. His breath was rapidly returning now, and he struggled with all his might, managing to catch one of the powerful brutes by the head in the crook of his arm. With a great twisting effort, he sent the half-naked body flying through the air. Then he was up on all fours, grappling with the other attackers. Powerful hands tried to close about his throat, but Hazard's right fist shot out.

Bam!

The blow struck with the force of a pile-driver; it should have sent the man spinning. But his assailant was no ordinary man; he only reeled back a step. As he came in again, the other brown-skinned devil was getting to his feet.

Now Hazard lost all sense of calm judgment; he became an utter madman. Mohra was gone, and these agents of Wu Fang were responsible for her leap into eternity. If it were the only thing he did on this Earth, he was going to avenge her.

Yelling like a lunatic, he tore into them, his movements so quick a motion picture camera would scarcely be able to photograph them clearly. He was ripping, tearing, digging, and gouging with insane fury.

Again and again, the man whom Hazard had knocked down yelled for pity. The other attacker had rushed in now. He seized Hazard from behind and raised him like a rag doll.

The place now seemed alive with yellow men. Some rushed in at Hazard; others clustered around Tanya and Rod Carson. When Hazard had last seen the young archaeologist, Tanya had still been trying to hold him up. But, now he must have slipped from her grasp, because neither of them was visible.

Other agents came rushing in answer to the screams from Hazard's assailant; he whirled to face them. His mouth was cut and bloody; his eyes protruded like those of a madman. A left in this yellow face. A right to that ugly brown body. A brutal blow to that slant-eyed devil over there.

Jerry Hazard moved like a streak of lightning. He fought on until fatigue overpowered him. His knuckles were covered with blood, bruised and battered. Suddenly everything seemed to close in on him. Although it was nearly dawn, darkness still blanketed the cliff. Then he was aware of only one thing. He heard voices, and he knew that he was being carried.

He opened his eyes in a room entirely strange to him. As full consciousness flooded back, he realized this must be the hiding place of Wu Fang. It was a great barren adobe chamber, without the heavy embroidered tapestries and gorgeous rugs that usually surrounded the Dragon Lord of Crime. There was a queer lighting effect, a strange lamp which was probably of Wu Fang's own design and which shed an unearthly lumination.

Wu Fang was standing in the center of the room, his yellow robe falling about him in majestic folds. The streamers on his small hat bobbed up and down as he gestured quickly with his head It was the first time that Hazard had ever seen the yellow devil in a violent fit of temper. He seemed to be upbraiding everyone.

Hazard's blank, staring eyes saw Rod Carson bound to a chair near him. Tanya was standing near Wu Fang. Strangely, she was not bound or held in any way, and there were no agents around her. To the left were some of the brown and yellow-skinned devils whose faces and bodies carried evidence of Hazard's insane attack.

Wu Fang was pointing a long-nailed index finger at the two brown-skinned bloody natives who had first attacked Hazard.

"Why did you let her jump off the cliff?" Wu Fang demanded. "Why did you permit her to go to her death? Do you think I hire you to kill the best agent I have? Do you think I will permit such a thing?"

One of them seemed blinded as a result of Hazard's attack. He was holding to the other one for support and guidance, but managed to bow, humbly.

"I am very sorry, Master," be said, "I tried my best to catch her."

Wu Fang whirled around to face Tanya.

"And you, my blue-eyed she-devil," he rasped, "why did you permit Mohra to jump off the cliff? Perhaps you thought that you would have first place in my affections if she were dead. Is that it?"

THERE was sorrow and pity in the great blue eyes of the flaxen-haired Tanya as she said, "No, Master. I am always your loyal servant. I did my best, but I could not catch her and stop Mr. Carson at the same time."

An agent spoke to Wu Fang in a strange, rasping tongue. When he had finished, the yellow fiend faced Tanya with a fiendish grin.

"Do you understand what Kuchdau says?" he demanded.

The girl's face went white, but she replied calmly, "No, Master."

"He says that he was watching you from the brush. He saw that you did not even turn your head to see where Mohra was, because you were too engrossed in easing Mr. Carson's fall to the ground."

The girl's expression never changed.

"Yes, Master," she admitted, "I was holding him in my arms. You remember, of course, that you put me in charge of the affair and made Mohra believe we were both being set free. You told me that I must be very careful not to use the perfumed handkerchief. I gathered, Master, that you wanted Mr. Carson kept in good condition for the experiment. That's why I lowered him to the ground so gently."

For a long moment, Wu Fang scrutinized the girl's face. Then a paternal smile spread over his countenance.

"You are telling the truth, my beautiful blue-eyed one," he said. "You have done your best and you are forgiven. I am greatly saddened to lose Mohra."

Jerry Hazard hadn't moved or uttered a sound but had been sitting there bowed down with grief at his loss. The whole affair was clear to him now. The girls hadn't been given their freedom; they had been sent down to the camp to lure Carson and Hazard to Wu Fang's hideout. Tanya had worked the scheme cleverly.

The yellow fiend swept his hand in a wide gesture. "Out, all of you!"

There was an immediate scurry for the exit. Tanya was last to go; Hazard, watching her, saw her glance quickly at Rod Carson. There was a strange expression in the girl's eyes, a queer mixture of remorse and satisfaction.

"You she-devil!" Carson gasped.

The girl flushed then quickly went out.

Wu Fang's green gaze swept from Hazard to Carson and back to Hazard again. He smiled now with that familiar fiendish grin.

"For once, Mr. Hazard, you and I have something in common. We are both stricken with grief for Mohra. But I am sure you will soon forget it, and I know I will."

Hazard's teeth clenched as he fought to retain some measure of calm.

"I have had you gentlemen brought here for a reason," Wu Fang continued.

"Yes," Carson said bitterly, "we know now from what Tanya said that we're to be used for guinea pigs in your experiments, the same way you treated Lahey."

Wu Fang chuckled. "Permit me to say that I have not used Mr. Lahey except as a patient under observation.

"You wrong me, gentlemen. I had you brought here for a special reason. It should be possible for us to cooperate on solving the secret of Suicide Tomb. Why was it called Suicide Tomb? Why should such a name be handed down from generation to generation?"

Carson and Hazard simply stared back at him.

"To all appearances," Wu Fang continued, "you know even less about it than I do, although you have spent much more time in the cave than my agent has. You have not, then, I assume, learned the mystery of the broken skulls."

"On the contrary," Carson exploded, "we have learned the secret. But you will never know it."

Jerry Hazard turned his head quickly to Carson and a look of warning flashed from his eyes. Carson was blundering; he didn't realize that Wu Fang would devise horrible tortures to make him tell what he knew.

Wu Fang turned toward the archaeologist quickly. "So you believe you have solved the mystery of the broken skulls, Mr. Carson?"

"Carson is lying," Hazard cut in immediately. "We know no more about the broken skulls than you do."

"I can easily tell when a man is lying." Wu Fang smiled triumphantly. "My perceptive powers have not weakened from the ravages of time. I believe, my friends, that I am about to show you something which you do not know."

He clapped his hands twice. A servant entered.

"Send Gunnar Drugge here," Wu Fang ordered.

The Scandinavian entered silently. He grinned at Carson and Hazard for a moment, then faced Wu Fang.

"What is the condition of my friend with the purple star on his forehead?" the Dragon Lord of Crime demanded.

"He is coming along nicely," Drugge answered. "But he will not reach the stage you anticipate for some hours yet."

"Good." Wu Fang nodded. "Then have Mr. Hazard and Mr. Carson taken out. See that they are bound securely and placed in one of the upper rooms. You will notify me when Mr. Lahey reaches the point in the experiment of which I spoke."

Gunnar Drugge bowed, went out.

"Look here, you beast," Carson choked. "I don't know what you are doing or going to do to Lahey, but I want to tell you this. He's a perfectly innocent man, and he's never done anything against you."

Four powerful, half-naked Malayans appeared as the yellow fiend answered.

"Mr. Carson, I believe that your friend, Mr, Hazard, can tell you that I perform my experiments on whomever it pleases me." His smile broadened. "Of course, I have an idea of vengeance in mind. You will know about that shortly. But it so happened that Mr. Lahey, having already been bitten by the white bat, fitted admirably into my scheme of experiments."

He nodded to the four foul-smelling agents who had entered the room. Two of them walked to Hazard and two to Carson. They picked the prisoners up, chairs and all, and carried them out of the room and up a flimsy ladder to the second floor. Without a word they brought them to a small room in the corner of the building and seated them, side by side, in a space between two small narrow openings that served as windows. There they were left alone.

Hazard surveyed the interior of the place. Aside from the two chairs to which they were bound, the room was merely an adobe square with two window-slits cut out.

Sounds of talk in a strange language came to them from far off in the ancient dwelling. A few moments later, the talk died away and there was dead silence.

Hazard managed to lean forward enough to see slantwise out through one of the window openings. He couldn't see their camp, for the window faced the wrong way, but it commanded a good view of the valley on the other side. Far off across the plain another range of cliffs towered majestically toward the sky.

Never had his thoughts entirely left Mohra. He felt weak and sick inside as he remembered the beautiful girl whom he loved.

"I can imagine how you feel, old man," Carson said sympathetically. "It's a tough break. She was *the* girl, of course?"

"Yes," Hazard admitted shortly, then fell morosely silent.

Carson tried to change the subject.

"What do you think he's going to do with us, Jerry?"

"I don't know. It doesn't particularly matter."

"Maybe it doesn't to you," Carson said, "but it sure does to me. Come on, old man, buck up. Remember, there's a lot more at stake in this situation than a girl. If Wu Fang is successful, there won't be a family in the world that can feel safe. I know you suffered an awful loss, and I'm mighty sorry for you. But now you've got to forget it. We must consider the rest of the people in the world and go on."

Despite his grief, Carson's advice filtered into Hazard's brain. He realized the young archaeologist was right.

"Yes," he said decisively, straightening from his slumped position. "You're right, Carson. I've got to go on in spite of it all."

CHAPTER TWELVE

The Madman

JERRY Hazard began twisting and straining at the ropes that bound him to the chair. He realized grimly that the men who had bound him were experts at the job. The more he struggled to get free, the tighter the ropes seemed to cut into his flesh. After a long struggle, he stopped, panting.

"How are you coming, Carson?" he asked.

"Not very well," Carson said, shaking his head. "We've got to go at this in a different way. Can you move your chair without making too much noise?"

Hazard leaned forward as much as his bindings would permit; his feet were tied to the front rung of the chair, but he managed to touch the floor with his toes.

"I think," he grunted, "I can shift around a little. Why?"

"If we can move our chairs so that we're back to back, we can work our fingers and untie each other. What do you say we try it?"

"I'll try anything," Hazard gasped. Head bent forward, feet barely touching the floor, he tipped his chair slightly, moving it a very little distance.

Carson's feet were bound on a higher rung so that his knees were directly under his chin; he couldn't reach the floor with his toes. But he began tipping his chair back and forth, swaying his body with what little freedom he had. The chair legs' clattered dully on the adobe floor.

"Careful of that noise," Hazard warned.

He managed to work his chair around inch by inch. It was hard, nerve-wracking work. Minutes wore on into an hour. He had moved about a foot in that time. Beads of perspiration stood out on his forehead. Both chairs were becoming rickety from the constant strain. Then there was a low grunt from Carson. Hazard turned. Horrified, he saw that the archaeologist had overbalanced his chair and was falling forward. His forehead struck the floor with a brutal blow; his body went limp.

"Carson! Carson!" Jerry whispered frantically. "Come on! Snap out of it!"

But Carson didn't answer. He lay limp and still on the rock floor.

Hazard stopped and tried to reconcile himself to the new situation.

Wu Fang's agents would be coming in at any moment. If they found Carson on the floor—

"Carson!" he called desperately. The still form didn't move. Was he dead?

Suddenly, Hazard realized there was no use in trying to work out the plan they had first devised. The only way he could get his hands on the ropes that bound Carson was to turn his chair half around again, move it back and tip it over sidewise. Then instead of the two chairs standing back to back, they would be lying on the floor on their sides with the backs together. That would achieve the same purpose; but to do that, Hazard would have to turn as far as he had already turned. That had taken him more than an hour. Still, there was no quicker way. He began straining once more at his bindings, stretching the tips of his toes to the floor.

Time sped on as he struggled desperately. After another hour's nerve-wracking work, he heard voices outside.

A slant-eyed devil's face appeared at the irregular door opening. Jerry Hazard tensed, then relaxed, waiting and motionless. The Chinaman grunted something and turned away. What did that mean? Was he going to tell Wu Fang that Carson had tipped over on his face? Would he suspect they were trying to escape?

The moment that the face was gone from the doorway, Hazard began working his chair again.

A faint groan came from the floor. Hazard turned, quickly. Carson was moving.

"Take it easy, old man," he whispered. "You're coming around now."

"My head," Carson groaned. "It feels as if it's going to blow up."

"Sssh!" Hazard warned. "I've just got in position to drop down beside you. We'll be untying these ropes before long. Don't speak above a whisper."

"How are you going to work it?" Carson asked, turning his head to look around.

"I've got to come around just a little more," Hazard said. "It's awfully slow work, but we can't help it. When I get around there, I'm going to tip sidewise. That will put us back to back. Then, I think I'll be able to reach the ends of the ropes around your wrists."

"Good," Carson said. "Fire when ready."

After a few more minutes of desperate straining, Hazard managed to rock his chair over on one side and fall to the floor behind Carson with a clattering sound. Then he was feeling for Carson's hands where they were tied behind his chair.

He found the knot. His numb fingers worked at it frantically. That knot certainly was tight. Now it was loosening slightly. There, he had the first knot untied. Now he was working on the second. He tore at it desperately; but it was even harder than the first.

What was that sound? Someone coming? He tensed a moment, listening. It must have been his ears playing tricks on him. There was no sound now. Again he struggled with the rope. Then the sound came a second time, a soft padding, like bare feet walking on the floor outside the room. If he could only get Carson loose! There, he had that knot now!

Carson's hands were moving; his wrists were spreading apart. He was shaking off the bindings that held his body to the chair. In a wild scramble, Carson rose, flung his own chair and the ropes that bound him off, and bent down behind Hazard. The newspaper man felt him working frantically at the knots above his wrists.

Still the padding of bare feet could be heard outside.

"Hold everything," Carson hissed. "I've got one of them. Press your wrists close together. Don't pull them apart until I tell you to."

Hazard pressed his wrists together as tightly as he could. His nerves were taut, ready to snap with the awful suspense.

"Got another one," Carson said.

Pad! Pad! Pad!

The sound was coming closer now.

Suddenly, Hazard felt his wrists free. Now, Carson helped him loosen the bindings that held his legs and body to the chair. He was trying to stand up, trying to restore the circulation in his limbs.

A sudden cry of alarm came from the door. Immediately there were shouts from other parts of the building and the sound of running, bare feet came louder.

"Carson!" Hazard shouted. "Out of the window, quick! I'll follow you."

"No," Carson shouted back. "I'll get you free first. Come on. Two more ropes. Out you go!"

Carson sprang for the window while Hazard was throwing off the last of his bindings. The archaeologist's foot caught in a loop on the floor as he dashed past Hazard's chair, tripping him and at the same time jerking the rope that Hazard was trying to throw off all the tighter.

A snarling, foul-smelling figure lunged through the air over them, crashing Jerry Hazard down. The shouts of alarm were almost deafening now.

As Carson struggled to rise, two half-naked devils landed on him, crushing him to the floor in spite of his valiant efforts.

Hazard tried to rise, tried to fight off his assailant; but others were there. His arms were pinioned behind him, and they jerked him from the floor and dragged him out of the room. As he turned quickly and shot a glance at Carson, he saw that the young archaologist, too, was being carried out.

AT THE top of the ladder in the next room, where it led down to the first floor, their captors stopped. Now the chairs were brought out and ropes were tied around them again, fastening them even more securely than they had been before.

Wu Fang greeted them with a fiendish, triumphant smile as they were brought down the ladder and set before him.

"You thought you would escape me," he chuckled. "I know you have done it before, Mr. Hazard, but that will not happen again. Now, I am ready for you to see the end of the experiment with Mr. Lahey."

As though to punctuate his words, a wild, fanatic scream sounded from somewhere outside. It was a cry of torment and awful agony.

"You may tell them to bring Lahey in," Wu Fang commanded.

"You yellow devil," Rod Carson spat. "Is that Lahey making those sounds?"

"Yes," Wu Fang said calmly, "that is Mr. Lahey. He has gone mad. I intend to turn him loose in this room and see what he will do."

"Why, you—" Rod Carson began.

But the screams from the Westerner cut off his words as they echoed weirdly through the ancient adobe building.

Jerry Hazard couldn't help cringing slightly at those sounds. He turned his head to stare behind him, and the sight caused phantom fingers of ice to play up and down his spine.

Lahey was being dragged in by two Malayan giants, and although each held one of Lahey's arms outstretched in front of them, their strength was tested to the utmost to hold the raving man, whose forehead was still marked with the purple star.

Now and then as they dragged him forward, Lahey's arms contracted as though he were trying to reach his head. In doing that, he almost flung his guards off their feet. Then he made a savage lunge forward, apparently not noticing anyone in the room.

He seemed in an awful torment that drove him on to something— heaven only knew what. In a sudden burst of violence, he swung both his guards around and started dragging them with him toward the nearest rocklike adobe wall at the end of the room. His head was lowered and he was charging like an angry bull. The guards struggled to hold him back.

Wu Fang uttered a sharp command. "Let him go."

Jerry Hazard caught his breath in a gasp as he heard that order. Let him go! Were they going to let that raving maniac loose in there? Was Wu Fang going to permit Lahey to murder them while they were bound help- less to their chairs?

The two guards released Lahey's arms and leaped hack. The Westerner, who had been leaning forward, straining as though to reach that nearest wall, rushed like a missile shot from a cannon. His head was still down like that of a mad, charging bull. Roaring and bellowing insanely, he raced on toward the wall. There was sharp crack—a splintering of bones.

Hazard shuddered and closed his eyes for an instant. When he opened them again, Lahey's body lay twitching, two or three feet from the wall where the force of the blow had bounded him.

Blood ran from his head, coursing over his neck and shoulders. Hazard couldn't see the skull, but knew that it was crushed from the awful blow. The horrible realization of the secret of the Suicide Tomb was clear to him now.

"You see," Wu Fang said smoothly, "I have just demonstrated how three hundred and ninety-six ancient people died of the plague. This explains the arrangement of the skeletons in Suicide Tomb. The plague acts upon the brain, causing such terrific torture that the victim's only thought is to bash his head to pieces and end the suffering. That is why the ancients, confined in this tomb by a wise ruler who wished to prevent the plague from spreading, all crushed in their skulls. It is most interesting, is it not?"

"It's devilish!" Hazard snapped.

"It's the most damnable thing I've ever heard of in my life," Carson said.

"To me," Wu Fang smiled, "it is a marvelous discovery. Think how it will aid me in my aim to become the ruler of the world."

"You will never get away with it," Carson rasped. "You may kill us but there will be others who will prevent you from accomplishing your ghastly aim, and in the end they will burn you. They'll hang you. They'll—"

"They will not have the opportunity." Wu Fang smiled calmly. "You see, my friends, I am already developing an innoculation that will control this plague. I will afflict those whom I wish with it, and the others I will render immune. The nations of the world will be delighted to grant me whatever concessions I desire to save their peoples from being destroyed."

With a sudden rustling of his yellow, silken robe, Wu Fang whirled toward a cage of white bats which Hazard and Carson had not noticed before.

"And now," the yellow fiend said, "it is time for the experiment upon you, Mr. Hazard, and you, Mr. Carson. I will now open the slats of the cage and permit the bats to attack you."

He lifted the bat cage, brought it over, and set it on the floor in front of his two captives.

"You see," he continued, "I want to know if everyone is affected by the plague. I have my own theories on that subject, but I wish to have actual proof."

He smiled now in his fiendish manner, standing by the cage with his hand poised on the first slat. The straining, fighting bats were leaping inside the box.

"You will assist the bats greatly by holding your heads still," he said.

Then he began drawing out the first slat.

CHAPTER THIRTEEN
Red Man's Vengeance

VAL KILDARE and Cappy had taken the first plane out of Newark airport for the West. They reached Tombstone from the nearest airport on the transcontinental line and hired a car to take them to the scene of Rod Carson's explorations into the Suicide Tomb. Strangely enough, although there had been no curiosity seekers following the expedition out beyond Tombstone, everyone seemed to know the location. The news had spread rapidly from one of the crew who had returned.

It was late afternoon when they arrived at the camp. Apparently, it was deserted; but after a few moment's search, Kildare spied a slant-eyed Chinaman coming from one of the tents. Instantly, the government man's hand flew to the butt of his automatic. He didn't draw it out, however, as careful scrutiny convinced him that the man was perfectly docile.

"You clum see Mr. Clarson?" the Oriental asked in a monotonous, sing-song voice.

"Yes," Kildare said. "Where is he? And who are you?"

"I am Ah Yung," the Chinaman said. "I am cook for Mr. Clarson. Not know where master go. Two lady clum early this morning. Very pletty young lady. Mr. Hazard, he hug one of them. Give her very big kiss. They talk in tent. Then they go away with two pletty young lady."

"That was early this morning?" Kildare demanded.

"Yes, velly early this morning," the Oriental assured him. "Was still dark."

"Did you hear them say where they were going?"

"Hear them say something about Chinese named Wu Fang. Ah Yung think Wu Fang very bad man."

"I'll say he is," Cappy cried out. "We know him, don't we, Mr. Kildare?"

Kildare nodded. "Did the four of them go alone?" he asked.

"No, three men go with them. Three men of party. One man die here last night and one gone away, nobody know how. Another one—he got light hair—he not come back to supper last night."

"Wait a minute," Kildare said. "Let me get this straight. First, one left and didn't come back to supper last night. You haven't seen him since?"

"No," the Oriental said, shaking his head. "Not see him again. He was velly big man. Got light hair. Named something like Glugge. He take up dynamite to cliff last night. Ah Yung think he try to blow up Mr. Hazard and Mr. Clarson. Mr. Clarson come back and say find him; but nobody find."

"All right, we've got that checked off. Now let's hear the rest of it. What happened when the man was killed and another one disappeared?"

"Man that disappeared—his name was Mr. Lahey—white bat bite him on forehead. Make purple, five-point star."

Kildare blinked and shook his head.

"I'm afraid you'll have to go a little slower, Ah Yung," he said. "You've left me way behind already."

"Those white bats, they say they find in cave up there on side of cliff. We catch them. Velly bad purple skeletons up there in cave. Hundred thousand skeletons, maybe million skeletons. Ah Yung not count them."

"In the cave? You mean the Suicide Tomb that I've been hearing about?"

"You good guesser. Lots of people die up there maybe thousand years ago."

"All right. Let's forget this cave business for now. You found some white bats up there. You brought some down and one of them bit Mr. Lahey. Is that right?"

"That light, mister."

"Then what happened?"

"Mr. Clarson and Mr. Hazard, they send Mr. Lahey to his tent. Tell him to go to bed. So Mr. Lahey go to bed in tent. Then comes ball of fire like velly tired sun from mouth of cave. Everybody shout and run out. Ball of fire disappear and ghost come out of cave and go around in front of cliff. Hear shouts and yells from tent where Mr. Lahey and Mr. Shorty sleep. Find Mr. Shorty lying in much blood. Mr. Lahey, he gone. Cage of white bats, that gone too."

"All that happened last evening?" Kildare asked.

The Chinaman's head bobbed up and down. "Yes," he said. "Last night. Then velly pletty girls come this morning before sunrise. Not hear what they say."

"And you haven't heard anything from Carson or Hazard since?"

"Nobody come back," Ah Yung said with a hurt expression. "Ah Yung get breakfast ready; nobody eat him. He get lunch ready; nobody eat him.

Now pretty near time get supper. Nobody eat him either." A ray of hope gleamed in the yellow man's eyes as he asked eagerly, "Maybe you stay supper?"

But Val Kildare didn't seem to hear him. His eyes were fastened to a movement of the brush out on the plain, perhaps two or three hundred yards away. Cappy and Ah Yung followed his gaze.

"Maybe they come back now," Ah Yung suggested hopefully. "Maybe everybody come back supper tonight. I hurry get ready."

"Gee, Mr. Kildare," Cappy ventured, "that isn't a whole party coming. I can tell that. It looks like just one person coming through the brush."

"That's the way it looks to me, too," Kildare admitted, whipping out his automatic. "I don't know who it is, but we're going to meet him half way."

But suddenly, as they advanced, Kildare saw a figure loom out of the brush; heard a hoarse, plaintive cry.

"Help! Help! Help!"

It was a girl running toward them; a girl whose dark hair was dishevelled, her clothing torn to shreds, revealing ugly, deep cuts and bruises on the white skin of her body.

"Mohra!" Cappy cried. "Gee, Mr. Kildare, it's Mohra."

The girl staggered a few steps forward, stopped and clutched the brush for support, as Kildare raced to her.

"Good heavens, Mohra," he exclaimed, "what's happened to you? Where are the rest of them? You look as though you—" He broke off abruptly as the girl fainted in his arms.

Kildare picked her up and ran back toward the camp, where he bathed her brow and face with water Ah Yung provided.

"She's been through a lot," the government man said, "but I think she's coming around all right."

As he spoke, Mohra's eyes opened and stared frantically for an instant. She raised her right hand weakly, but when she clutched Kildare's hand, her grip was firm.

"Oh, Mr. Kildare." she gasped, "we've got to hurry. Something terrible has happened to Jerry and Mr. Carson. And it was all my fault. I led them into the trap without knowing it. Tanya—"

The girl stopped and gasped for breath.

"Where are Hazard and Carson?" Kildare demanded.

Mohra's voice choked and her eyes filled with tears as she continued,

"They are prisoners of Wu Fang—" she pointed to the great cliff where the ancient pueblo stood— "up there. He is going to use them for his experiments as he did Mr. Lahey."

"Lahey?" Kildare cried. "He's the one who was bitten by the bat, isn't he, Ah Yung?"

"Yes." Mohra nodded. "He's the one. I am sure of that. He was stolen from his tent down here, and now Wu Fang has Jerry and Mr. Carson."

"How did you get away?" Kildare demanded, almost savagely.

"I—I couldn't stand it," Mohra sobbed. "Wu Fang's men tried to catch me as I ran away. I knew Jerry would think I had deliberately tricked him into going up there, and I could never face him again. I jumped off the cliff."

Kildare's eyes widened in amazement as he repeated incredulously, "Jumped off the cliff?" He pointed to the great ledge rising a thousand feet or more. "You mean you jumped from the edge up there," he asked, "and you're still alive?"

"Yes," the girl cried, sobbing heart-brokenly now, "but I wish I hadn't lived. I can never face Jerry again. I was just getting to the point where I could fight off Wu Fang's influence, but now—now Jerry will think—"

"Don't you worry about Jerry," Kildare snapped. "Leave him to me. The first thing we've got to do is to get Carson and Hazard out of that jam. Is anybody else with them?"

"No, no," the girl sobbed. "Only Tanya, and she's still under Wu Fang's spell. She'll do anything he tells her."

"Do you know the way up the cliff?" Kildare demanded.

"Yes," Mohra said, "I know the way."

Kildare stared down at the girl's body. Her clothing had been torn in places and there were deep gashes and bruises on her arms and legs.

"I don't think you could stand it," he said. "Can't you tell us the way? Cappy and I will make it. We've each got a gun and—"

"No, no," Mohra protested. "I've got to go with you. You will need me. Maybe I can get a gun here and help you. I've got to go, I tell you."

Kildare began bathing the wounds on her body with the tepid water Ah Yung had brought.

"I can't understand," he said, "how you could possibly live after a leap like that."

"I—I don't know either," the girl admitted. "All I remember is that I closed my eyes so that I wouldn't know when the end came and leaped. After a minute I hit something. It was a narrow ledge; there was a small cave by it, and I crawled into that. I had sprained my ankle and couldn't walk, but when daylight came I managed to hobble around a bit. There was a passage from the cave leading back to the ledge. I crawled through it and got down the trail."

They stopped to listen as Mohra finished. A strange sound had reached all their ears; a grunt, that was animallike and yet held a human note. Then another grunt, accompanied by the sound of footsteps, padding softly towards the tent. Kildare whipped out his automatic and faced the entrance.

Ah Yung had spun about as a head appeared at the flap of the tent. It was the head of an Indian, with strange streaks of paint on his face.

"Who are you, and what do you want?" Kildare demanded.

"You come out," the Indian suggested. "We make talk."

"Good," Kildare said, "You've come just in time, too. We may need some help."

"What do you mean—help?" the Redskin demanded as Kildare stepped from the tent.

"I'll tell you as soon as I find out what you want," Kildare replied.

The government man surveyed the camp with astonishment. A few minutes before it had been entirely deserted, now it was completely surrounded by young Hopi braves. In the center of the group was a young Indian with blurred, wattery, sightless eyes, holding to the arm of a squaw who was apparently guiding him.

The Hopis were armed with rifles, and as they closed around him, Kildare realized he was helpless.

An elderly Redskin with a wrinkled, aged face came before him.

"I am the uncle of Sitting Fox," he said, turning and pointing to the young Indian in the center. "Sitting Fox is our chief. He has suffered much at the hands of white and yellow men."

The old Indian paused to appraise Kildare's companions. Cappy was beside Kildare, unafraid. Ah Yung was on his other side, staring in squint-eyed perplexity at the group of Indians. Mohra remained just outside the tent opening.

"And now," the old uncle said impressively, "we have come for revenge."

Revenge! Kildare realized immediately the answer to all this. These hundred-odd Hopis had been outraged. Each face reflected its intense hatred of the white man.

"I believe I know what you mean," Kildare said. "But first I want to make it clear that none of us know anything about it. We are after the same yellow fiend as you. Let me talk to Sitting Fox so I can find out exactly what happened. You must act quickly if you're going to catch the man who is to blame."

"We have come to the right people," the uncle insisted. "There is no need to talk to our chief. We are sure."

Then the blind young Indian called out, "Let him come and talk to me."

Obediently, the Indians cleared a path for the government man who approached their chief.

"You were the young chief who took his grandfather's place as head of the Hopi tribe not long ago," Kildare began. "I remember reading about it in the paper. You were given a secret map showing the location of the Suicide Tomb on the cliff."

"That is right," Sitting Fox said. "I gave the map to Mr. Carson, the explorer, thinking he would be able to learn more about it, so the true story of the Suicide Tomb might be handed down through the generations of the Hopi tribe."

The old Indian standing at Kildare's elbow cut in, "And it was Mr. Carson who turned against you. We do not know why nor do we care, but you—" He pointed to Kildare. "you are Mr. Carson, or a close friend of his, and we will get revenge from you."

"I am a friend of Mr. Hazard who is now with Carson," Kildare corrected.

"You are the one who is to blame," the old Indian repeated. "You and the Chinaman. The boy, and the woman have also helped."

"You are wrong," Kildare said. "Sitting Fox will tell you so himself, I believe."

"How can he tell?" argued the old Indian. "He's blind."

"Yes," Kildare nodded, "but he still has ears; and if he's a good Indian, he can remember voices. You have heard me speak, Sitting Fox. Have you ever heard my voice before?"

"No," Sitting Fox said, shaking his head. "I have never heard your voice before."

"There," Kildare spoke triumphantly to the uncle. He turned again to the blind Indian. "What happened to you?" he asked. "What made you blind?"

"It began," Sitting Fox said, "when I was leaving Mr. Carson's house, the night I gave him the map. When I left, it was dark. I was walking through the streets of Tombstone when suddenly I became paralyzed, and fell to the ground. I was caught by a man—a huge, light-haired man—"

"Was his name Drugge?" Kildare asked quickly.

Sitting Fox thought for a moment before he nodded.

"Yes," he said, "I heard his name spoken and it sounded like Drugge. He was the man who tied me on top of a great building in the garden outside the house. It was in a great city."

"In a house?" Kildare asked. "On a building? You mean a penthouse? A penthouse in Chinatown?"

"I don't know," Sitting Fox said. "I was paralyzed for a long time. I must have traveled a great distance. When I awoke, I was in a box like you use to bury your dead."

"It was a penthouse," Mohra breathed, excitedly. "Wu Fang had his headquarters in a penthouse on top of one of the large buildings in Chinatown, and he had an Oriental garden in there. I saw this man—"

She broke off suddenly with a gasp, for Sitting Fox had turned his face toward the direction from which her voice came and the sight of his horrible, running eyes sickened her.

"Then I can tell you what happened," Kildare said. "You were taken to Wu Fang, who's trying to learn the secret of the Suicide Tomb. He tortured you, tried to force you to tell him where the cave was."

Sitting Fox nodded without changing the expression on his face.

"Yes," he said, "that is correct. But I did not tell him. He tied me to the side of a lattice with my head bound so that the sun shone directly into my eyes. He propped open my eyelids with little sticks so that I could not close them; and the sun blinded me. I will never see again."

Kildare turned to the uncle who seemed to be in command.

"Wu Fang is now hiding in the ancient city of cliff dwellers high up on that shelf of rock. Let us go up after him together and finish him for all time."

"The white man lies," the old Indian persisted stubbornly. He whirled to his braves and shouted, "Capture these four! We begin at once our revenge for the loss of Sitting Fox's eyes."

Val Kildare tried to step back, but he found his arms pinioned to his sides. Two husky Hopis picked up Cappy, who struggled like a wildcat. Ah Yung and Mohra were seized roughly and dragged forward toward the center of the camp.

"You will be tortured as Sitting Fox was tortured," he declared. "But we will be good to you. Sitting Fox lives and suffers, but after your tortures, you will die. You will be burned at the stake."

CHAPTER FOURTEEN
The Flight of Wu Fang

VAL KILDARE was fighting for words of argument, fighting for some method by which he could prove their innocence.

"This is a civilized age you're living in," he said calmly. "People aren't burned at the stake any more. When the government of the great white fathers finds out who is to blame for our deaths, you will pay the penalty. Your lands will be taken away from you, and you—"

The old Indian stepped quickly before him as he spoke and struck him a brutal blow across the mouth.

"You will say no more," he commanded.

With tent ropes, the Hopis bound them to separate posts. The Chinaman was babbling frantically in his native tongue, and his yellow face had taken on a white, pasty look as he realized what was going to happen. Cappy uttered no word, but his eyes stared desperately into Kildare's as though he were saying, "Gee, Mr. Kildare, can't you think of anything that will stop these guys?"

Kildare was racking his brains desperately to find an argument that would have some weight with these half-mad Indians.

"The man you are after will escape," he repeated, "before you have time to reach him. He's up there on the cliff. We will help you in your vengence against him."

"Mr. Kildare is telling the truth!" Mohra cried out. "I know. I have been an agent of Wu Fang. I was at the penthouse when Sitting Fox was blinded. That is the truth, no matter what you think. You are killing four innocent people. Up there—"

"Don't talk!" the old Indian grunted savagely. "That is proof that you are one of his accomplices. You even admit it. Light the fire so that these people will be tortured as Sitting Fox was tortured."

The pile of dried twigs that was now heaped about Kildare's feet up to his knees was crackling. But he was still trying to think of some last argument that would save them before the flames and smoke would screen them off and close their mouths forever.

Suddenly, Sitting Fox spoke.

"She is right. She is not lying. I recognize her voice now. She pleaded

with the Chinaman to spare me. She tried to help me when I had nearly gone blind. Put out the fires and release these people! I know they are telling the truth."

"No," the old man disagreed. "Do not believe him."

The voice of Sitting Fox rang out now in sharp command.

"I am blind, but I am still your chief. I have given an order. Put out the fires and release them. We will go to the cliffs to seek vengeance against the yellow man who is to blame. Your chief has spoken."

Instantly, Hopi braves kicked the blazing sticks away from the feet of the four prisoners, then untied the tent ropes that bound them.

"Come on," Kildare announced. "The girl and I will lead you. She knows the way to the ancient dwellings of your ancestors." He turned to the girl. "Do you feel strong enough, Mohra?"

"Yes," she nodded eagerly. "But we must hurry."

WHEN THEY reached the bottom of the trail, they were forced to break into single file. Kildare's automatic came out now, ready for action.

"You've shown us the way to the trail," he said, turning to Mohra. "I'll lead now. We're going to strike trouble from here on, and I'm going to take the brunt of it. Jerry would want me to."

Halfway up the perilous path, Mohra cried, "Look! Look up there! That large pueblo on the cliff! Do you see it?"

Kildare strained his eyes in the direction she pointed and nodded.

"Yes," he said, "there's somebody watching us from an upper window." He spun to the Indian in front of Cappy and pointed. "See that figure up there in the window of the largest pueblo?"

The Indian grunted. "Yes. Want me hit him with my rifle?"

Kildare nodded. The group moved on as though they hadn't noticed the face at the window. Kildare saw the Indian bend down, even as he was walking. He moved the gun swiftly to his shoulder.

The government man had his eyes glued to the window. At the crack of the rifle the head loomed up higher in the aperture. Then the body tumbled out in a wild leap.

"That will warn them that we're coming," Mohra protested.

"They know it already," Kildare assured her. "This will let them know we're here for business. Come on."

Up and up, over the edge of the giant rock shelf, and all the while Kildare's eyes searched the brush, where agents of Wu Fang might be hiding with strange beasts, with blow pipes and poison darts.

But there was no sign of moving sage or rabbit bush ahead. No yellow or brown heads peered through leaves. No beasts of death flung at them. The way seemed clear . . . left open for them. Kildare moved more cautiously. It wasn't like Wu Fang to show no fight.

The brush was passed. Nothing had happened. The largest of the dwellings on the cliff was directly before them. Mohra, who was running close to Kildare, pointed at the structure.

"That is the place," she said. "You enter by a ladder which leads to the second floor, then down into the first floor."

The Hopi Indians saw the ladder at that moment and rushed for it. But Kildare's long, fast moving legs beat them to it. He went up, rung after rung. Hopis followed directly behind him, fairly pushing him on ahead.

Kildare reached the edge of the second floor window opening and leaped into it with one mighty lunge. Finger on the trigger, he was ready to shoot at the first sign of any of Wu Fang's agent. The room was barren.

He dashed into the next room, where his keen eyes caught sight of a hole in the floor and the ladder that protruded through the hole.

Bending over, he yelled down into the dark interior.

"We've got you, Wu Fang. Might as well come out in the open and surrender peaceably. There's a hundred Indians here—"

His voice broke off sharply. From the weirdly lighted lower room, a cry came to his ears. Not a cry of pain or fear; rather, the voice expressed warning.

"Quick, Kildare. He's gone. He's gone with his agents to the Suicide Tomb. He's gone for—"

The voice died, as though the speaker had been attacked.

Kildare recognized the voice instantly. It was Jerry Hazard speaking.

While he had listened, his eyes became accustomed to the strange dimness of the room into which he stared. He made out two figures below him, both bound to stout folding chairs.

In that same quick glance he saw something white swoop from the darker recesses of the ceiling for Jerry Hazard's head. It was a diving white bat. With a violent movement, Hazard fought to escape the bat's attack. The chair to which he was bound was hurled over backward by his violence, and he went crashing to the floor.

He landed on one shoulder and with his hands behind him. He could control his rolling movements a little by pushing with his bound wrists against the floor. The white bat seemed to sense the danger of being struck by the struggling feet of Hazard. Or perhaps it was startled by the sudden action of the newspaper man. At any rate, it spread its wings and shot upward once more. At that moment a hurtling body came through the opening in the ceiling. Hazard saw it was Kildare, gun in hand.

"I'm coming, Jerry! Keep kicking!"

Kildare's feet struck the adobe floor with a thud. He was up and running for Hazard and Carson—and the white bat.

In the meantime, the winged demon had gathered courage for another attack. It circled with a quick flip of wings and dived again. This time it went for the newcomer who now menaced it.

Kildare crouched as the bat dove at him. He was holding his fire. Holding it so long that Hazard yelled:

"Shoot! Shoot!"

As though Kildare had been awaiting the command, his gun boomed the answer.

Bam! Bam! Bam!

Flame darted from the muzzle of his automatic. But still the bat came on. Kildare took aim again. The gun bellowed out, the dank smelling room shuddering with the blasting sound. This shot went home.

Before Jerry Hazard's eyes the white bat vanished, as though a magician's wand had swept it clear. Then Kildare was tearing at the ropes that held him.

"Any more bats in here?" he demanded calmly.

"No," Hazard said. "That one got out just as Wu Fang received news of your arrival. He closed the cage then and gave orders to catch more bats and escape before you could reach here with the—"

Hazard broke off as he was helped to his feet by Kildare. And while both bent over to untie Carson, Hazard demanded:

"What's all this we heard about Indians coming with you?"

Kildare explained briefly. When Carson was released, Hazard introduced them.

WHILE the fight with the bat was taking place and the two prisoners were being set free, Sitting Fox's men had been pouring into the lower room. Now a half dozen Hopi Indians were gathered around them menacingly.

Kildare whirled on them.

"The man we're after has fled," he explained. "Quick! Up the ladder to the second floor. He's gone to the Suicide Tomb!"

The Indians grunted and turned. With Hazard and Kildare and Carson on their heels, they climbed the ladder. As they attained the second floor, Kildare turned to Hazard.

"Know how we found you here, Jerry?"

Hazard hesitated for an instant.

"No, I hadn't had time to—"

Hazard broke off as Val Kildare smiled. Frantic hopes rose in his heart.

"Mohra told us," Kildare said. "She's alive."

"Mohra!" Hazard shouted, his heart pounding double time. "Alive! Where?"

Kildare smiled. "We left her outside."

As Hazard's feet struck the ground, Mohra rushed to him, arms outstretched. Joy overcame Hazard as he realized that Mohra and he were together again. Only that.

"We're going on, Jerry," Kildare said. "Perhaps you and Mohra had better stay here."

Hazard felt Mohra push him away.

For an instant, duty and desire tangled; but he shook his head.

"I'm going too," he said. "Got to see it through."

Mohra understood.

"Yes," she said. "Wu Fang must be stopped. Nothing else matters until that is accomplished."

Next thing Jerry Hazard realized, they were following the Indian guides down a thickly grown trail, leading to the smaller shelf of rock below, in front of the mouth of the Suicide Tomb.

Hazard never took his eyes from Mohra on that downward descent. He guided her, helped her from rock to rock. All but carried her over the more precarious places.

A deathlike stillness hung over the great plain, which to Hazard was appalling. He knew from the orders Wu Fang had given that he and his agents were going to the Suicide Tomb, and he felt sure that there would be plenty of traps for any who tried to follow him.

The Dragon Lord must have gone to the lower shelf of rock by some other path, Jerry reasoned. By some mysterious and secret way that he had divined in his weird cunning. For if they had passed along this trail, they would surely have been seen by Kildare and the others as they came up to the rescue.

Hazard stole quick glances up the cliffs as they crawled along. Surely the center of that cliff was too steep to be scaled except by this path. But some of Wu Fang's men could climb up the side with ease. Those same ape beings had done much more dangerous climbing—up sheer walls of buildings in the city. This would be simple for them. And a loosened rock or so sent hurtling down might cause a slide that would carry the entire searching party with it.

A Hopi Indian in the lead let out a cry of victory as his feet touched the small ledge. He ran headlong for the mouth of the tomb, darted inside. A moment later he came out again.

"Nobody in cave! Cave empty!" came the shout.

Kildare spun round and ran to the ledge of the shelf.

"They've gone down by the trail, then!" he yelled. "Come on! If you see anything moving, shoot to kill!"

Jerry Hazard broke away from Mohra for an instant to stare over the edge of the shelf, far down into the valley.

"Kildare," he said, "the trail is empty. I can see it from here."

He had left Mohra close to the face of the cliff, a few feet from the cave entrance. A shrill cry suddenly reached him. His blood chilled. He whirled.

The sight that met his eyes made him gasp in horror. A rope dangled out of the half darkness from a point more than a thousand feet above. And at its very end, some twenty feet above the ledge, were two human beings.

A small brown beast of a man with a grinning face and powerful arms, clutched the rope with his left hand; the loop ran around one leg, at the top, making a sling by which he hung. The right arm of the devil was around Mohra.

"Jerry! Jerry!" she shrieked. "Stop him! Stop him!"

Scarcely realizing what he was doing, Hazard dashed ahead until he stood directly under the dangling forms. Suddenly, Kildare's voice commanded.

"Shoot them down. Don't hit the girl. Cut the rope."

Now the rope was being hoisted rapidly. Two Indians raised their rifles.

Crack!

Crack!

But the brown little demon was clever and managed to keep the girl's body well in front of his own. Forty feet!

"Mohra! Mohra!" Hazard found words. But they were pitifully inadequate. "Kick. Get—"

Mohra was going away from him. It seemed to Hazard that the higher the rope was drawn, the faster it rose.

A cry of fear blurted from the newspaper man's lips as another shot cracked out. For an instant the two forms, dangling fifty feet above the floor of the shelf, seemed to stop.

The bullet had clipped one of the strands of rope; but the rest of the rope was holding. And the brown fiend, with Mohra still struggling in his one arm, was going up, up.

"Stop firing!" It was Carson who uttered that quick command.

Sixty feet up!

"If you cut that rope now, she'll be killed when she falls!"

"I don't care!" Mohra screamed down. "I don't care! Anything is better than going back to—" Her words ended in a choked gasp as her body went limp. That was almost the last thing that Jerry Hazard remembered. He began searching blindly toward the cliff. It was almost vertical, but he'd climb it somehow. He had to climb it.

Then the world grew hazy, and he was conscious of nothing.

"Jerry. Got to keep calm. Don't let it get you, old man. Jerry! Jerry!"

Wam!

Jerry Hazard was dimly aware next of a stinging blow across the face. Things grew clear and he saw Kildare before him.

"You damn near went nuts," Kildare warned. "Tried to get up the cliff after—after Wu Fang."

Instantly Hazard was himself again. He stared about wildly.

"Where is she?" he demanded. "Where—"

Kildare's hand was on his shoulder. "Take it easy, old man. There's nothing we can do from here. She's—"

Hazard didn't need to catch any more of that. He saw a speck high up against the cliff.

"What—" he groaned— "what can we do?"

Kildare spun to the Indians. "Any of you know the way to the top of the cliff? The shortest route?"

There seemed to be a difference of opinion as to the best course. Kildare's lanky body stiffened.

"I have an idea," he said. "Wu Fang came down here to collect bats from the cave. Isn't that what he ordered, Jerry?"

Hazard nodded.

"Then I'm going to take a look in the cave. Come on. I've got a hunch that Wu Fang reached the top of the cliff from the inside of the tomb."

"What?" Carson and Hazard exploded in the same breath. But Kildare was already running inside the cave ahead of them. He produced a flashlight from his pocket and snapped it on. The strange musty odor of the death chamber reached Hazard's nostrils as they ran, the Indians coming on behind them.

Kildare made a circuit of the round walls.

"Look, Jerry," he said. "Was that there when you were here before?"

Hazard's eye's stared fixedly at a break in the wall of the cave. Carson's voice cracked out in the semidarkness.

"No," he said. "I'm certain that opening wasn't there before. Look." He pointed to a slab of rock lying on the floor. "That wasn't there, either, when we were here. Remember, Jerry? The skeletons were all out in the clear. And now this stone slab is lying on three of them."

Hazard suddenly leaped ahead toward the opening. It was narrow and came to a point at the top, like an inverted wedge.

"There's a draft," he stated excitedly. "That means that this passage leads someplace on the outside. Come on."

He sprang forward, with desperation driving him on. Mohra was up there near the top of the cliff; there might still be time to save her. As he broke through the opening and felt his feet pounding the steep incline, Kildare called savagely:

"I'd like to know how that yellow devil found this opening. It must be centuries old. Look!" His flashlight played on the soft earth that floored the narrow passage. "Footprints! They're all tangled up. Bare feet, most of them."

The floor tipped up at a steeper angle. The turns of the passage grew less acute. Then Hazard's straining eyes saw something up ahead—a tiny round twinkling light.

"A star!" he exclaimed. "We're almost at the exit!"

A rumbling sound of triumph came from the throats of the Indians. Then all that was changed. A voice, horribly familiar, cooed down the passage.

"You have come just in time to see Mohra lifted over the cliff. But you will never see her again. I am taking her with me, this time as my slave to do with as I wish. I hare all the white bats from the cave. All of them." He laughed again. "We go at once to my headquarters in Chinatown from where I shall spread the purple death in New York. The plague will spring up. Nothing can stop me now. People by the thousands will be bashing in their heads against buildings in less than a week."

"Wu Fang, you yellow devil!" Kildare yelled, "you won't go through with it. You don't dare!"

But Wu Fang was laughing down at them. They could hear the cackle of his voice as he said:

"You will know nothing of the outcome, unless it is possible for one to see from Hell. I now give the command."

There was a moment of deathly silence.

"Perform the mass execution!"

Hazard struck out with a final burst of speed. He could see other stars through that opening just ahead. Then, one of the stars was blotted out. And another and another. He heard Kildare's automatic bellow almost in his ear. But the great shape at the mouth of the rock crevice came on. Some great object was charging down upon them. An object that filled the passage. It was a boulder, he realized, and they were trapped in its path!

CHAPTER FIFTEEN
The White Bats Strike

A GIANT transport plane burst out of thick clouds several hundred feet above the Newark airport, giving Val Kildare, Cappy, Jerry Hazard and Rod Carson their first glimpse of the lower New York City sky line.

"Gee," Cappy said, "when that rock was falling down on us I never thought I'd see this again."

"We all thought that, Cappy," Kildare smiled. "And if that boulder hadn't been so large, we wouldn't have."

"Wu Fang over played his hand for once, thank heaven," Carson observed. "If that boulder had been six inches smaller, it wouldn't have jammed in the narrowed neck of the crevice just ahead of us."

The plane was landing. Jerry Hazard had said little during the entire trip from the west. Again and again he had gone over the horrible disappearance of Mohra.

Passengers were leaving the plane as Hazard got up with a jerky motion. Never once did the thought of his job or his office in the news syndicate enter his head. He had made up his mind to one purpose. Whether Kildare thought well of the idea or not, he would go to Chinatown. He would search every corner of the city until he found Mohra.

A police touring car with top up was parked close to the waiting room. An officer in the blue uniform of the New York police was just getting out. He walked toward the plane.

"You're Mr. Kildare?"

"Yes, Sergeant, what is it?"

"Captain McGuire of Mulberry Street sent me to watch for you and hurry you into town as soon as possible," the officer explained.

Kildare was already striding toward the police car. He made short of the introductions.

"I'm Sergeant Ryan," the officer said and opened the car door.

"Now, tell me more about this, Sergeant," Kildare said, when they were under way.

"Something queer is happening," the sergeant explained. "We got a tip that Wu Fang came in on a little field over in Long Island. We've kept watch in Chinatown since then, but couldn't spot anything. Then this afternoon, a guy comes running out of a house on Mott Street. His head's all bloody; he grabs it with his hands, lets out a yell and runs across the street. He's got his head down like he thinks he's a billy goat. And I guess he was pretty sure of it, for he smashed his head into a brick building. Broke his skull. And I hear the plain clothes men sayin' that you could see his brains through the busted bones."

"What was the number of the house on Mott Street?" Kildare asked, leaning forward just a little.

"Twenty-one," came the answer.

"Will you take us there at once?" Kildare asked.

"Yes, sir. That's what I was figurin' on."

"Where's McGuire?" Kildare asked.

"He's down in Chinatown. Got a sort of headquarters set up in a place at the back of 19 Mott Street. That's right next door to the place the guy came out of. I suppose you want me to drive you to him first thing?"

"Yes." Kildare nodded.

IT WAS nearly dark as the car swung into Mott Street. Hazard was half out of the car before it stopped, with Kildare bounding after him. The sergeant uttered a warning.

"I wouldn't make too much fuss," he said. "Might make the Chinese suspicious."

"You mean," Kildare hissed, turning, "that you've got a hundred plain clothes men stuck about Chinatown, and the Chinese haven't suspected something going on?"

Sergeant Ryan grinned. "They're pretty foxy," he admitted, "but we think we've got 'em guessing this time. Follow me. I'll take you to McGuire."

The sergeant stepped to the door at 19 Mott Street and turned the knob. The door opened easily.

Hazard's nostrils were instantly aware of the strange, Oriental tang in the air. A very narrow hall led to a stairs that creaked in warning as they climbed three flights.

"McGuire has gone up in the world since I saw him last," Kildare observed as they topped that last rise.

"He's got a place up front where he can watch everything in the back yards," Sergeant Ryan explained. "We're right there now." He motioned to a door ahead of them. "He's in that room there. Keeps it dark—so he can see without being seen."

Eagerly, Jerry Hazard stepped forward. The door opened slowly. McGuire put his face to the dark opening.

"It's Sergeant McGuire. Kildare and his friends are here."

A low answer came from the dark interior.

"Show them in. Tell them not to make a light. I'm watching something strange out back."

The sergeant stepped aside. Hazard pushed through the open door. He wasn't sure, but he thought Cappy came behind him. Then someone else. Vainly, Hazard tried to see in the darkness.

Blam!

Out of the abrupt silence, the sound that came from behind was like the bursting of a bomb. There was a quick, scuffling step. Then the door, that had just been open behind them, banged.

"Jerry!" It was Cappy's voice. "We're trapped. Somebody swung the—"

Thud!

Carson was pounding on the other side of the door.

Then from behind came a nerve-shattering chuckle.

Instantly Hazard recognized the laugh of Wu Fang, mocking them in the dark.

Bam!

The place was suddenly illuminated with light. At the same time Hazard was seized from behind. Strong hands held him motionless.

The keen eyes of the newspaper man took in the room. Walls were covered with the finest and sheerest of silk, worked in intricate designs of the greatest delicacy. On a low teakwood table stood a rough wooden box. Inside, he could see clawing white bats, anxious for their release. A Chinese girl with the sweet face of a twelve-year-old angel stood beside the box, smiling. She held a string in her hand that could snap open the front of the bat cage.

Wu Fang stood a little to the side of the room, holding in his hand a little vial of liquid. He too was smiling.

Cappy and Carson were struggling, each between two of the stinking, half-naked Malayans who pinioned their arms from behind. Kildare was nowhere in the room.

Wu Fang was speaking.

"Do not worry about your friend, Mr. Kildare. I will have him brought in presently. In the meantime, I will explain to you."

"You yellow beast," Hazard yelled in sudden mad rage, "what have you done with Mohra?"

"Mohra," Wu Fang smiled, "is well. However, I will not guarantee that she remains that way."

As Hazard opened his mouth to answer, the hand of one of his captors was clamped over it.

"You are to be highly honored," Wu Fang continued. "You and your friends are to be among the first to be afflicted by the plague of the white bats."

The thin, sloping shoulders of the yellow fiend shook with mirth.

"And this that I hold in my hand." He held up the glass tube filled with liquid. "This is a cure for the plague. But it is only known to me. For I alone hold the secret." Again the beast chuckled. "After the bats have injected the plague germs into you, then they begin their work upon the innocent humans outside."

Insane strength came to Hazard in a rush of power. He whirled and at the same time leaped forward, wrenching his piniomed arms from those guards that held him.

He was suddenly free. Free to leap forward at Wu Fang. Hands outstretched to claw and choke and tear, Hazard lunged across the short space that separated them.

Snap!

The cage door flashed open. And the eager, savage bats swooped with mouths open wide, purple teeth gleaming in the dull light.

In that moment of frenzy, Hazard's feet caught something. He never knew whether he stumbled or was tripped; but he knew he was going down, down.

As Hazard went down he knocked a diving bat from before his face. Then Wu Fang was suddenly flinging the vial of liquid he held in his hand. Flinging it at the bats which were coming toward him. He whirled and ran for a door.

"The odor. It did not work!"

That meant one thing to Hazard. The repellent odor with which Wu Fang controlled his death beasts had no effect on the white bats. And now Wu Fang was in as much danger of being bitten and struck insane as the others.

Carson and Cappy were suddenly free. Hazard leaped up from where he had fallen. With chairs and tables and bits of furniture, they fought off the bats.

The Chinese girl who had sprung the trap had vanished. Hazard didn't see her go. He dived for the door through which Wu Fang had vanished. A figure clothed in a yellow robe rushed into the room. It was Wu Fang.

Hazard made a frantic leap for him. His hands were on the scrawny wrist of the yellow fiend. With incredible speed, Wu Fang whirled for just an instant. The long nails of his other hand stabbed down like talons.

Hazard swung his left fist. But in that same quick move, Wu Fang darted away, and Jerry Hazard suddenly found that he was powerless to hold to that wrist. Something had happened to his right hand and arm. All feeling was gone from it.

Bam!

From behind came pounding feet and shouts as the police stormed in with Val Kildare leading the way.

Hazard bounded back from the panel through which Wu Fang had just passed.

"Wu Fang—" he panted—"just went through—there!"

Hazard reeled against Kildare. "I had hold of Wu Fang," he gasped. "Couldn't seem to hang on. I'm going numb. He—scratched me with his nails."

Dimly, he heard Kildare say, "A drug. It'll wear off. I'll be back."

As Kildare lunged through the opening with the blue-uniformed officers, things grew very dim to Jerry Hazard.

A soft voice was floating gently in his ears, and as Hazard came back slowly, he saw Mohra bending over him. They were in an ambulance. No, they weren't either. They were in the back seat of a police car. He was half reclining in Mohra's arms.

"Never, Jerry," she was saying. "We'll never be separated again, darling."

"Did they get Wu Fang?" Hazard demanded, suddenly aroused.

"They have him cornered," Kildare said. "It's just a matter of time. He's trapped three flights below Chinatown."

Jerry Hazard turned his head toward Mohra. Their lips met. Hazard was weak but that wasn't the only reason he closed his eyes as they held that lingering kiss. It was because he didn't ever want it to end.

THE END